Readers love
SJD PETERSON

Remember When

"This is a love story that spans decades. If you like friends to lovers stories, then this one is a must."
—Sinfully: Gay Romance Book Reviews

"This book spoke to the unwavering romantic in me! It's a story of how young, first love really can be the love that lasts a lifetime."
—Diverse Reader

Something's Brewing at Joe's

"It gripped and held onto me with its hot and sizzling chemistry, its humorous and sexy bantering, and its kept-me-on-the-edge-of-my-seat suspense. I love, love, loved it!"
—Gay Book Reviews

Limitless

"I recommend this to everyone who's intrigued with BDSM, the Dom/sub relationship, the concept of pain mixed with pleasure, and flawed, realistic men who more than deserve a happy ending."
—Long and Short Reviews

"I would definitely recommend this book!"
—Alpha Book Club

By SJD Peterson

Published by DREAMSPINNER PRESS
www.dreamspinnerpress.com

Romance Redefined

SJD Peterson

DREAMSPINNER
PRESS

Published by

DREAMSPINNER PRESS

5032 Capital Circle SW, Suite 2, PMB# 279, Tallahassee, FL 32305-7886 USA
www.dreamspinnerpress.com

Romance Redefined
© 2017 SJD Peterson.

Cover Art
© 2017 Reese Dante.
http://www.reesedante.com
Cover content is for illustrative purposes only and any person depicted on the cover is a model.

ISBN: 978-1-63533-807-2
Digital ISBN: 978-1-63533-808-9
Library of Congress Control Number: 2017904710
Published November 2017
v. 1.0

Printed in the United States of America
∞
This paper meets the requirements of
ANSI/NISO Z39.48-1992 (Permanence of Paper).

To all those struggling to keep it together.

CHAPTER ONE

THE STENCH of stale alcohol and sex hit me before I even opened my eyes. I lay there for several moments trying to figure out what was happening and hoping it was nothing more than the lingering effects of a bad dream. I knew it wasn't, but I was holding on to the possibility a bit longer because reality was seriously going to suck. My bladder, on the other hand, had other ideas. It wasn't going to allow me to hide. Slowly I opened my eyes and blinked several times until they adjusted to the bright sunlight streaming into the room. The bedroom looked like a tornado had touched down: pictures on the wall tilted, lamp overturned, clothes scattered, and shoes tossed aside with abandon. All proof of a night of poor choices, and if that wasn't enough, the rumbling snoring sounds coming from next to me surely were. I turned my head toward the noise and slapped a hand over my eyes. *Oh, you did it this time, Ben. You lost your goddamn mind.* I splayed my fingers, took a quick peek, and groaned. Lying next to me in all his naked glory was my exhusband, Hugh Bayard.

The weight of the situation crashed down on me like a ton of bricks, and I couldn't get out of that bed fast enough. I stood beside the mattress, staring at Hugh, trying to get a grasp on how in the hell I'd come to be in bed with my ex. Then the thick alcohol-infused cloud lifted and the events of the night before came rushing back with humiliating clarity. Hugh's invitation to dinner, the drinks— far, far too much alcohol, then… I groaned again. What an idiot. I knew better than to drink to excess, especially around Hugh. We sat at the restaurant, eating, drinking, laughing. I remember the tingling, thinking this wasn't going to turn out well, then the next thing in a taxi heading to my place. Kissing, hands roaming over warm skin, clothes falling away….

How could I have been so stupid? I'd done the one thing I swore I would never do again—let Hugh Bayard back into my bed.

Embarrassment, irritation, and regret increased by the second. Then, just to add the cherry to the top of my emotional cocktail, I had to look at Hugh again. Even in sleep, the man looked polished. His dark salt-and-pepper hair, cut short enough that there was no bed head, his neatly trimmed beard, streaked with silver, accentuating his strong jawline. His features lay slack, giving him a softer look. If it was possible, Hugh looked even better asleep. Suddenly, without waking, he rolled, covering his head with the sheet. Irritation filled me again, and I snapped out of my lustful thoughts. How appropriate—Hugh Bayard turning his back on me after he's fucked me.

I snatched up what clothes I could find and stomped into the bathroom. I gave in to the demand of my bladder, then took care of whatever had crawled into my mouth and died during the night. Minty fresh, I left the bathroom without a glance at my reflection. I was pretty sure I wasn't going to like what I saw. Instead, I ran my fingers through my knotted hair, smoothing it down best I could. No doubt, I looked like a crazy man, but I didn't care. Hell, it was only appropriate—I had the crazy all over me.

For once, my poor housekeeping skills were a bonus because I found my unfolded laundry in a basket on the coffee table. I rummaged through it, found clean underwear and jeans but no shirt. I searched the area—*aha*—my shirt from the night before was on the floor near the closet. I grabbed it, shrugged into it, and instantly regretted the decision. The cotton material still smelled of Hugh's rich scent, which just irritated me all the more. It didn't matter that I was just as guilty of the epically bad decisions. Hugh was the one who brought out this side of me. This was all his fault, and now his scent was all over me again. I hated it, but I'd rather cut off my left nut than go back in the bedroom and take the risk of facing Hugh again.

I found my sneakers beneath the couch and jammed my feet into them without socks. I found my wallet on the kitchen counter and shoved it in my back pocket. After one last look around, I fled the apartment. It was going to be a long, long workday, but first, I had to find something for the throbbing in my head or the day wouldn't only be long, but painful.

THE FIRST hour at the Common Cure, the local restaurant and bar I'd been lucky enough to get employment at when I'd first come to the city, was pure hell. The drumbeat in my head had quieted, but that left me with nothing to do but focus on the bad choices I'd made. *Epically bad choices*, the little voice in my head clarified, whom I just as quickly told to shut the fuck up. Thankfully, around eleven, the lunch rush picked up before I could go completely insane. It was all I could do to keep up with the crowds rushing in with the hope they'd make it to the front of the line before their lunch break ended. The mass of people fighting each other for a meal during a New York City hour boggled my mind. Hadn't anyone ever heard of a frickin' sack lunch?

"Hey, Ben. What's up?" Melanie, or Mel as I so fondly called her, popped up next me to check out the crab salad I was making. "You've been distracted all morning."

"No, no, really. I'm just peachy, nothing going on with me," I grumbled without looking up. I couldn't meet her gaze. She'd know something wasn't right. She had an irritating way of knowing when I'd fucked up.

"Doesn't sound like nothing is wrong, so spill it," Mel insisted.

"I'd really rather not."

"Too bad. You know I won't let it go until you tell me," Mel said, sounding determined.

That was okay—I was just as determined not to get into it. I wiped my hands on my apron, then made the mistake of glancing at Mel. My resolve faltered. Mel and I had hit it off instantly when we first met, even with our ten-year age difference. Melanie Knutson, with her blonde curls, bright blue eyes, and turned-up nose, looked much younger than her twenty-four years. However, beneath that sweet appearance was a motivated, single-minded, and dogged spirit intent on changing the world one goal at a time. Not only did she work full-time at the Common Cure, but she also took a full load of college courses, determined to be a social worker someday. Mel had grown up in foster care and was appalled by how some of those who were supposed to protect children failed miserably. She wanted to make a difference and was a huge advocate for reform to the current system. I had no doubt she'd do remarkable things.

"What happened?" Mel insisted. When I remained silent, she added, "Come on, Ben. I can tell you're dying to get whatever it is off your chest."

"I totally fucked up!" Robert, the dishwasher jerked his head around to gawk at us. Great! I gritted my teeth and lowered my voice. "I did something really, really stupid."

"You didn't call for bail money, so I seriously doubt it's that bad."

"I wish it was as simple as needing bond." My body heated as unwanted memories from the night before flooded back. Hugh kissing me, fumbling hands on zippers and buttons. Skin, heat, pleasure…. I gave myself an internal shake. Mel was a good friend, but I had to get myself back in the present. I was sure she wouldn't have appreciated me popping a boner while she was grilling me. I shoved the unwanted images away and took deep breaths, trying to get myself under control. I stole a glance at Mel, who was still staring at me with an expectant expression and tapping her foot impatiently.

"Fine! I slept with my ex last night," I blurted.

Mel's eye went comically wide. "What?"

She knew all about my disastrous marriage to Hugh. God, I couldn't count the number of times I'd sworn to her that I wouldn't touch Hugh again, not even with a ten-foot pole, so it was no wonder she was staring at me in shock.

"I know, I know. Hugh showed up unannounced, informed me that my mother is getting married. I mean, I was skeptical. I totally wouldn't put it past my mother to make something like that up just to get me to come home. You know she just can't seem to help herself from trying to find ways to dig her controlling tendrils back into me. But my mommy issues are for another time." I blew out a pent-up breath. "He got me drunk."

Mel arched her brows. "Sure he did."

"I'm serious, Mel, he did."

Mel waved a dismissive hand. "Whatever, Ben. Regardless of whether he did or didn't, I'm insanely jealous right now."

"About what?" I asked incredulously.

"You told me your ex is hot, hung, and rich." Mel tilted her head, a blonde curl falling into her face. She blew it out of the way before saying, "On second thought, I think I kind of hate you right now. Do you know how long it's been since I've gotten any action?"

"No, and I don't want to know, so zip it." I scowled at her. "But you're more than welcome to Hugh. Be my guest. Just let me know how great you feel after he bangs you, then turns his back on you once he's satisfied." I snapped my mouth shut as the anger began to bubble up.

"I'm sorry, that was insensitive."

Sincerity filled Mel's voice, but she really didn't understand my reasoning. Mel focused so much on her goals that she had no desire to tie herself to anyone. She had no problem keeping emotions out of the physical equation. Sex for pure pleasure and nothing more. God, how I wished I could do the same thing. If only I could have compartmentalized like that. Unfortunately, I'd been in love with Hugh since even before I knew what the meaning of love was. I'd never been with anyone but Hugh, and the thought of being with someone else in the future…. I really didn't want to think about it. "Apology accepted, but only if you'll cover for me this afternoon? I've got an audition."

"Seriously, Ben? You're going to use my insensitivity for your personal gain. That's low, man."

"Yes, I am," I told her and smiled broadly. "Now get back to work before you get us both fired."

"This isn't over," Mel assured me. Nonetheless, it was for now—she was forced to get back to work when the crowd continued to swell and the manager began to shout.

I STOOD outside the small rundown building and frowned. I checked the address again, and it was the right place. It wasn't Broadway—

hell, it wasn't much more than a community theater that looked like it was on the verge of being boarded up—but I was desperate. I'd take what I could get. I'd exhausted and embarrassed myself trying out for role after role. It was the same "don't call us, we'll call you" response each time. And those were the nice ones. I'd finally broken down and hired an agent—sort of. Frank Wolfe was new to the biz, still in the process of building his clientele. It was the only reason I could afford him. What Frank lacked in experience, he made up for in enthusiasm.

Hot musty air hit me when I opened the door, and sweat instantly bloomed on my brow. I pulled a napkin from my pocket and swiped it across my forehead, hoping to look less rattled than I was. In the main theater, there were row upon rows of scarred wooden seats sloped toward the stage. The carpeted aisles were threadbare and stained. The place was nearly as shabby as my apartment, and it didn't smell any better either. Even so, the familiar reactions that any theater evoked in me kicked in. My pulse sped up a notch, and butterflies took flight in my stomach. The place may not have looked it, but to me it was magical. I'd experienced the same reaction when my parents took me to my first Broadway show as a kid. I sat between them in awe, captivated by the lights shining on the stage, the glittering costumes, and the amazing backdrops. The actors onstage danced to the orchestra's movements and melody, even when only speaking. Every detail of that enchanted night imprinted itself on my young mind. A dream sparked inside me, and I knew someday I would be an actor.

I studied the group of people milling around the stage. Maybe this was my chance. I squared my shoulders and walked confidently down the aisle. I'd put my dreams on hold for far too long.

An older woman, overly dyed red hair pulled into a tight bun with pencils stuck in it, sat at a table with papers scattered across it. She looked up when I approached, her lime-green glasses perched precariously on the tip of her narrow nose. She looked like she belonged there in that theater, quite the colorful character. She raked her eyes up and down me with a disapproving expression. "Honey, you're about ten years too late for the starring role." She chomped her gum, popped it noisily, then went back to rustling through the papers in front of her. "Next!"

Story of my life. Honestly, the blame sat squarely on my shoulders. I was kicking myself in the ass for not going after my dream sooner. I'd waited too long. "Umm, ma'am?"

She lifted her head slightly, her lips pursed. "You're still there."

"Yes, ma'am. Is there another role I could read for? I'll take anything."

She studied me for a moment, her expression not softening in the least. I held my breath, and sweat rolled down my temple. It felt like an eternity but was, in actuality, only seconds before she said, "Fine. I suppose you can read from the uncle's lines."

My heart started beating again, and a smile stretched my face. "Thank you."

"Don't thank me yet," she said flatly. She rummaged through the papers before her and thrust out a crumpled stack. "Here's the script. Start at scene two. Mike will read with you." She pointed toward a metal chair on the stage. "Have a seat."

I took the script with a shaking hand. I glanced at the paper, and for a moment, it looked like it was a foreign language. My excitement instantly turned to apprehension. I squeezed my eyes shut for a second, then studied the paper again. Oh, thank hell, I could read it, but the mini-freak-out had shaken me. My legs were trembling when I climbed the steps to the stage. Thankfully, I didn't make a fool of myself and fall on my ass. Yet, with the way my throat was constricting, I wasn't sure I'd be able to speak. A tumble down the stairs didn't seem all that tragic right then. I forced my feet to move. I could do this. I took the chair as instructed and swallowed down the lump of fear in my throat. *I can do this*. Saying it enough times might make it true.

Mike, an older gentleman with a thick gray beard and sour expression, came to stand next to me. He started reading, but he was mumbling so badly, I was having a tough time understanding him. I said a little prayer and then scanned the script, trying to figure out where we were at and where my cue was. However, I missed it, because Mike cleared his throat and nudged my arm. I automatically started speaking. My voice was flat, and I sounded as if I was reading from an instruction manual rather than becoming the character. I tried to capture the essence of the uncle, but it was in vain. No matter how hard I tried, I simply wasn't feeling it. Somehow, I got through it. The scene ended and I looked toward red-haired woman. By the way she was looking at me with a bored expression, I'd bombed miserably.

"Next," she called.

Dejected, I left the theater. I'd never sucked that bad at an audition, including my first, which was really saying something. It had to be the reappearance of Hugh that had thrown me off so badly. It was the only explanation. My acting teacher had been a godsend, and with her help, I'd made great strides. It had to be Hugh's fault. He had strolled back into my life, messed with my head, and shredded my confidence.

Bastard!

CHAPTER TWO

I LEANED my head against the bus window and watched the landscape fly by in a blur of color. I dreaded each mile. I didn't want to return to Charleston. While I was looking forward to seeing my family, I would also have to face Hugh.

Dammit, why had I let Hugh seduce me? In irritation, I shut down my Kindle and stuffed it into my messenger bag. I'd spent the entire journey from New York to Charleston thinking about Hugh Bayard. What a stupid way to spend my time. Hugh wasn't worth it. Twenty-two wasted hours I could never get back.

The bus maneuvered the narrow streets of Charleston, South Carolina, and I pushed Hugh's memory down and tried my best to concentrate on the beauty of the town I'd grown up in—the grand historical homes that lined the road, the manicured lawns and array of colorful blooms—but the stunning beauty of the town wasn't enough. The painful truth: Hugh was never far from my thoughts.

It seemed not that long ago that the touch of Hugh's lips and the caress of his hands had branded me in some irrevocable way. Perhaps I resented Hugh for that more than anything else. In spite of Hugh's emotional distance, he'd been a very good lover. Too good. Could I ever find another man who could compare with Hugh that way? Perhaps I should try. I needed a comparison, or at the very least someone to fuck the memory of Hugh right out of my head.

The bus came to a stop, and I had to force myself to exit with the rest of the passengers. I was tense, my movements jerky, and my ass hurt from so many hours sitting on it. The stench of diesel fuel wafted up around me as I made my way into the station with a messenger bag and one small suitcase. I didn't plan to stay long. A few days—then back to New York and on with my life.

"Hello, Ben."

I whirled around toward the unmistakable voice of my ex and glared at him. Why did he have to be here? Couldn't the bastard have given me at least a little more time to get my shit together before facing him? Apparently not. Because Hugh was standing there, wide smug grin on his all-too-handsome face.

I continued to glare at him for a few heartbeats, then abruptly turned my back on him. Not the most mature thing to do, but I needed a second, dammit. Unfortunately, it did no good. The tension tightened in me like I was an overwound clock. The sensation increased exponentially as I felt Hugh's gaze boring into me, cranking and cranking that damn clock mechanism. Just when I thought my goddamn head would explode, Hugh came around to stand in front of me. I struggled to present an aloof facade but was sure I failed miserably.

"Hello, Hugh," I said stiffly. "I didn't expect to see you here."

Hugh smiled wryly. "It's good to see you too, Ben."

"Don't be so condescending. I would think being snobbish is beneath you."

"It is, and I'm serious, it is good to see you. I never got a chance to say goodbye the last time," Hugh drawled in that infuriatingly sexy, slow manner of his.

"Still, you managed to leave your message." I rummaged inside my messenger bag, found the envelope, and thrust it at Hugh. "There. I'm returning your money." Suddenly I was as furious as I'd been when I'd found it tucked under my coffeepot, like he was leaving payment for services rendered. I was pissed.

Hugh stared at the envelope. "I just wanted to help out. After seeing how you live, it doesn't—"

I held up a hand. "Just take the goddamn money. I don't need nor want your handouts."

Hugh hesitated but then took the envelope without saying another word. The silence stretched out uncomfortably. It only fueled my irritation, and I couldn't help but throw another jab at Hugh. "If you're taking time away from the office, Mother must have bribed you to retrieve me like a good little puppy," I said snidely.

"No, I volunteered to pick you up. I thought we could finally clear the air about a few things," Hugh said calmly.

Either Hugh was oblivious to my irritation or didn't care. Of course, that just pissed me off all the more. "I don't think there is anything to clear up. I'd be okay if we agree to never speak again."

"Aww, c'mon, Ben, you don't mean that. Here, let me take that for you." Hugh took my suitcase before I had a chance to reply. I clenched my jaw to hold back the curse and followed him. While my stride was stiff, Hugh strolled with grace and confidence. My gaze was drawn to his firm ass as it swayed with each step. I tried not to appreciate such a fine backside, but it was impossible. I'd never been able to resist Hugh's sex appeal. He was tall with broad shoulders, a lean waist, and well-defined muscular legs—all the things I found attractive. Even during the difficult times in our relationship, I couldn't help but crave Hugh. The physical aspect of our relationship had never been a problem. It was the affection that was lacking. Hugh rarely shared his feelings. Always having to guess and wonder what the man was thinking and feeling was maddening. In the end, I ran. Cowardice, perhaps, but I didn't really have a choice.

Hugh tossed my suitcase into the back of his SUV, and I slid into the passenger seat and stared straight ahead. A few seconds later, Hugh got us on the road. "It's a little stuffy in here," Hugh said and flipped on the air conditioner.

"I think it's fine." I shut the air vent on the dash in front of me. Sweat trickled down my spine shortly after, and I grudgingly opened the vent again.

"Why do you have to do that?"

"Do what," I snapped without turning away from the window.

"Argue with me."

"I don't do it all the time."

"Sure, you do," Hugh said with a hint of amusement. "We'd go out and you'd insist on being the one to pay the tab. You'd argue with my opinion about a concert, a movie, or a book. You'd argue with me about anything and everything. Hell, I swear you liked to argue just for the sake of arguing."

I tensed. I'd been so young when I'd fallen in love with Hugh. Young, in love, and at the same time, needing desperately to declare my independence. From the beginning, Hugh's powerful personality had inspired both fascination and rebellion in me. It made for a volatile combination.

"I remember you enjoyed goading me, just as you're doing now," I grumbled.

"Aww, Benny, would I do that?"

I turned my head just long enough to roll my eyes at him before staring back out the window. *Benny.* Hugh's private name for me, a name no one else had ever used nor would I have allowed anyone else to. I made an effort to concentrate on the scenery instead of how my stomach fluttered.

The downtown streets behind us, we drove along the water's edge. A few people were out walking on the beach. Gulls soared effortlessly on the breeze, and the sun glinted off the waves. I tried to enjoy the scene. I'd always loved the ocean, but I couldn't relax. Hugh had a way of doing that to me.

Before we made it to the Winthrop mansion, Hugh pulled off the main road and down a narrow dirt one. I gritted my teeth. I knew exactly where we were going and what his plans were. We'd spent plenty of time at the abandoned farmhouse, just sitting around talking. The last damn thing I wanted to do was talk to Hugh. Apparently, he had other ideas, because at the end of the drive, he cut the engine. He stared out the window, gripping the steering wheel tightly. His jaw set in a hard line.

The tension within the small space grew until it was almost suffocating. I rolled my neck, but it did little to ease the strain. When I could no longer stand it, I glanced over at Hugh. "If you're going to talk about the other night, don't. There is absolutely nothing to say."

"Look, I agree things got carried away. I didn't mean for that to happen."

"You and me both," I grumbled.

"I would have told you if you hadn't run."

"Hugh," I warned.

The muscles in his jaw twitched. "Fine. What I meant to discuss with you is your family. Regardless of whether we get back together, what you're doing to them isn't right. You can only use me as an excuse for so long."

"You did not just say that to me!" When Hugh didn't respond, I narrowed my eyes. "Are you fucking serious? You wanted to lecture me about my family?"

"Wow, is that what you've been doing in New York? Improving your vocabulary?"

"Just one of many things I've been doing to improve my life." I didn't have to justify anything to Hugh.

"Improve your life?" Hugh laughed. "I've seen where you're living. It's horrible, Benny, and so are the excuses you're making for not coming home. You're hurting your family."

"That's the key word, Hugh. *My* family and I will deal with *my* family in *my* own way."

"I just don't want you to stay away from them because you're mad at me."

"You!" I laughed without mirth. The sound was strangled by bitterness. "You are such an arrogant bastard. Have you ever thought that maybe, just maybe, I'm doing this for me?" I threw up my hands in frustration. "Never mind. You never listen, so what's the point?"

"That's not true, Benny."

"Yes, it is. I've tried talking to you, tried explaining why I was unhappy and what I needed. It did no good, so I don't see the point in rehashing it."

"This is about my job, isn't it? You always resented how many hours I had to work."

I shook my head. "Here we go again down the same damn path. I know what Bayard Investments means to you, but the long hours you put in were only a part of our problem." Those old feelings of hurt bubbled to the surface, as raw as ever. I wanted to scream, to make Hugh listen for once, but knew it would only end in disappointment. Hugh was the typical "macho" man. He had a hard exterior, not

13

allowing anything or anyone to penetrate to the soft parts within him. It had astounded me when I learned how Hugh spoke highly of me to others, but never once did Hugh ever, ever relay those feelings directly to me. He never said he was proud of me, never complimented me. He only said "I love you" when he felt obligated to repeat it.

"Then tell me. Explain the other problems, and let's work it out," Hugh said calmly.

That damn calmness turned my hurt into rage. "Stop it! Just fucking stop it, Hugh. You know damn good and well what I've told you. You either ignored me or didn't care enough, so just stop it!"

Hugh stared at me, and I held his gaze unflinchingly. Hugh started to open his mouth, then quickly shut it again. For the briefest second, I thought I saw pain, maybe regret, in Hugh's dark eyes. Then, just as quickly, it was gone, and the mask of indifference was firmly back in place. "I care very deeply."

The first thing to pop into my mind was to tell him just where he could shove it. The right words were coming out of Hugh's mouth, but they sounded flat. Typical, unemotional Hugh. I was wasting my breath. The worst part, I'd let my emotions get the better of me and allowed Hugh to witness how much he could still affect me. "Yes, I'm sure you do," I finally told him. "You know what I care about at the moment?"

"What's that?"

"Going to Mother's, getting a shower, and getting some clean clothes on." All those hours on a bus left me exhausted and stinky. I wasn't in the mood to rehash old shit. My head throbbed. As angry as I was, I couldn't deny the desire that still swirled inside me. The passion reawakened. I still wanted Hugh, still longed for his touch. I hated feeling that way but had no idea how to change it. My only choice was to stay far, far away from Hugh Bayard. "Are you going to take me home, or should I walk?"

I placed my hand on the door handle. Hugh must have realized how serious I was, because he nodded, started the engine, and put the car in gear. I watched out the side window as the old farmhouse disappeared from view. Nostalgia tightened my chest. This used to be our place, somewhere we could come for privacy and shut the world out for a while. Now it was just an empty field and a rundown shack. Nothing more.

Not wanting to stroll in the past any longer, I focused on the present. "I hear you've been dating?"

"Do you believe everything you hear?" Hugh countered.

"No, but I believe the photographs I've seen in the *Charleston Society Times*." I refused to look at Hugh or acknowledge the jealousy that shot through me every time I'd seen a picture of Hugh with his arm around yet another handsome man or woman. Actually, I'd been surprised to discover that the photos of Hugh with a beautiful woman on his arm bothered me the most. I'd always known both men and women attracted Hugh. Perhaps he'd be more likely to find someone willing to play the role he wanted most among the women of Charleston. Hello, nineteen fifties. On the plus side, he wouldn't have to go through the hassle and expense of adoption or of hiring a surrogate.

I really was losing my mind. Why did I care who Hugh was with? It was over between us. I'd moved on. I was living my life for myself and no one else. And dammit, I was pretty sure if I said it enough times, I'd even start to believe it.

"Does it bother you?" Hugh asked, pulling me from my musings.

"No, not at all. I was merely making conversation." The lie flowed from me easily. "You certainly didn't waste any time to get back into the swing of things."

"Why shouldn't I? You made it clear you wanted nothing more to do with me. You're still making that clear, even though you allowed me to share your bed."

Hugh was taunting me by bringing up my single night of indiscretion. I refused to let him bait me. I wasn't going to give Hugh the satisfaction of knowing that I knew he got some perverse pleasure out of it even if he wouldn't admit it. Hugh had always known my weakness, which hadn't been hard to figure out since it was the man himself. And sitting in that small car with him wasn't making it any goddamn easier to resist that pull.

15

Hugh turned off the road and stopped the car in front of the heavy iron gates that guarded my childhood home. He leaned out his window and punched a series of numbers on the security panel. A second later the gates buzzed and swung open.

I frowned at Hugh. "What the hell? I don't even know the security code anymore."

Hugh drove through the archway. The gate clanged shut behind us. "Why does it bother you that I'm still on good terms with your family? I've known them pretty much my whole life. Just because—"

"Don't say it," I warned. "Besides, I'm not saying you shouldn't get along with my family, only that I don't understand how you do. Constant meddling in my affairs means Mother and I can't spend more than a few minutes together before we're arguing."

"You should give her another chance. She's been quite upset since you left."

"I seriously doubt that," I said under my breath. Upset she couldn't control me, maybe.

Hugh stopped the car in front of the house—although perhaps "house" wasn't precisely the right term for such an ambitious structure. The Winthrop châteauesque mansion had been built in the late 1800s, at a time when my ancestors had harbored a fondness for French Renaissance châteaus, with their steeply pitched roofs, turrets, and sculptural ornamentation. Architecturally, the place was impressive.

Hugh sat with both hands resting on the steering wheel, tapping his thumbs. Funny that I couldn't wait before to get out of the small confines of the SUV, away from Hugh, but now I couldn't seem to move. I wasn't looking forward to an evening that would surely be highlighted by a blowup between Mother and me.

"Ben, is it really so bad coming home?"

"Yes. You know how Mother is. She can't help but push and push until I end up saying something she will try and use against me."

"I can go in with you if you'd like," Hugh offered.

I glanced at him, then shook my head. "It's better if I do this alone. That way there won't be any witnesses to where the body is hidden."

"C'mon, Benny, you know it's not that bad. She just wants you to be happy. We all do."

Meaning: as long as I do what they want. "I appreciate your meeting me at the station," I said stiffly.

"Well, aren't you just so polite."

I pursed my lips. "Yeah, well…. This place brings out the worst in me."

"I suspect you can handle your family. In a way, you handled all of us a year ago. This time just go a little easier on them, huh?"

I turned from him. How like Hugh to align himself firmly on the side of my family. That's the way it had always been. My entire family plus Hugh lined up against me. I scrambled out of the car. Before Hugh could join me, I made my way around to the back of the SUV and retrieved my luggage.

Hugh stuck his head out the window. "You sure you don't want me to come in with you?"

I shouldered my bag. "Nah, I'm good."

Hugh gave me a fleeting smile and then rolled up his window. I watched him disappear down the drive, suddenly feeling completely alone. I took a deep breath and turned toward the house. My nerves threatened to take over. My flight-or-fight response went nuts. Funny thing was, or perhaps not so funny, I regretted not allowing Hugh to shield me from what was about to happen. I supposed it was always going to be like that. I was learning just how hard old habits were to kick.

CHAPTER THREE

BENSON HOWARD Winthrop's stern face stared down at me from its rightful place, front and center above the mantelpiece. I never really knew my grandfather and namesake, but for as long as I could remember, the photo freaked me out. His eyes followed me whenever I was in the ballroom, and I avoided the room like the plague. I disliked the entire fussy room with its hard and uninviting furniture, huge floral arrangements, and gilded bronze statues. Mother knew I hated it, and yet her maid had ushered me in here almost half an hour ago. This was so typical of Mother. She was obviously trying to make a point. I'd left her, ignored her pleas, and she was going to try to make me suffer for my disloyalty. It wasn't going to work. I had a lot of guilt, but moving to New York City wasn't one of them. So I sat there twiddling my thumbs and waited for her to make a grand entrance.

At last, the tap of heels sounded in the hall, and Mary Grace Winthrop appeared in the doorway. She smiled graciously, as if I wasn't her only child but one of her socialite guests. I barely refrained from rolling my eyes. "Benson, my dear. Come give your poor old mother a hug." Mary Grace looked anything but old, and she damn sure wasn't poor.

A slender woman of fifty-six, Mother could easily pass for ten years younger. Her hair was dyed a dark auburn red, and her skin was still firm and barely lined, thanks to having Dr. Mack, her plastic surgeon, on speed dial. At times she'd try to come off as frail, but it was nothing more than an act to put others off guard. In reality, she was a shrewd, determined woman.

She held out her arms, and I went to give her a dutiful hug. A cloud of flowery fragrance engulfed me more powerfully than her dainty embrace. "We won't quarrel this time." Mother made a kissing sound near my cheek. "Absolutely not."

"We'll see how that goes, considering it was you who started the fight last time," I said, battling to keep the familiar annoyance out of my voice.

"Never look to place blame, dear. It's ungentlemanly." Her expression was one of indifference as she waved a dismissive hand, the same gesture I'd witnessed her give "the help" on numerous occasions. "Besides, I absolutely refuse to get upset today."

Thirty seconds in and she was already working hard to get under my skin. I refused to give her the satisfaction of knowing she was getting to me. I was exhausted from my long trip, and sleep and peace were my only concern. The quickest way to achieve that was to keep my mouth shut and let her do the talking.

"Come, let's have a chat." She gracefully lowered herself onto the sofa and patted the spot next to her. "You must be terribly surprised that I've decided to marry Charles."

"I'm very happy for you." I covered my mouth and stifled a yawn.

"You know, Ben, I've been foolish to make Charles wait so long. I'm glad I've finally made up my mind to go ahead. And that brings us to the subject of you and Hugh."

"Here it comes," I said under my breath. The tension instantly kicked into high gear. Another mother-and-son fight was imminent.

Mary Grace settled back in a corner of the sofa. She brushed a delicate hand over her chiffon skirt and then folded her hands in her lap. She completely ignored my obvious discomfort. "I want to know how you've reacted to seeing Hugh," she said. "Let's be frank, dear. Don't tell me the experience didn't affect you."

I struggled with another surge of annoyance. "Mother, how many times do I have to tell you it's over between Hugh and me? I didn't appreciate you sending him to New York to tell me about the wedding. A simple phone call would have sufficed."

Mary Grace shrugged one shoulder. "I just think you ought to get your feelings out in the open. Let's be honest. You can't deny that Hugh is someone special."

Usually when Mary Grace said "Let's be honest," it meant that she wanted other people to be honest, leaving her free to pass judgments and proffer advice. It was particularly irritating when the subject turned to Hugh.

I stood abruptly and went to stare out the window. The lawns were expertly manicured and, in my opinion, as cold and as uninviting as the ballroom. Everything was too perfect, untouched, as if no one ever strolled across them. Mother had tried to do the same to me, clean me up, put me on display to be appreciated and envied like her Louis XVI china. A crack in that perfection had formed when I told her I was gay. However, when Mary Grace had learned of Hugh's sexuality, she was hell-bent on seeing us together, to form an alliance. That was how the Winthrop family viewed it all those years ago—an alliance, not a romance. Two of the wealthiest families in Charleston united, her social status taking a hit but not destroyed. It was why she wouldn't be satisfied until she accomplished a reestablishment of that alliance.

I turned away from the window and faced her again. "Mother, you have to stop. You have to accept the truth about Hugh and me. It's over."

Now Mary Grace assumed a philosophical air. "You're just kicking up your heels a little, that's all. You never had a chance to be on your own before you settled down with Hugh, so you're doing it now. You just have to get it out of your system."

"I'm not getting something out of my system, as you so politely put it. I'm building a life for myself."

"One you're quite mysterious about, if I do say so. What do you do, Benson? I'm aware you haven't touched any of the funds in your accounts. How on earth do you support yourself?"

I refused to answer that question. My family wouldn't understand or approve of me working in a restaurant, living in a dive, or my aspirations to be an actor. I wasn't doing anything "expected" of someone of my breeding, and I secretly enjoyed the hell out of it.

"Mother, I'm doing just fine. You don't have to worry about me."

"Well, I do worry." Mary Grace gazed at me in consternation. "I always hoped that you and Hugh would discover the joys of parenthood together. That would've anchored you, given you purpose. And Hugh would be a wonderful father."

"Unlike me, right?" My voice tight as I struggled to get my anger under control.

Mary Grace paused, apparently considering her words carefully. "Benson, please do not put words in my mouth. I don't understand where all this hostility is coming from."

"It's not hostility, Mother. It's frustration. I'm a grown man and yet you still insist on treating me like a child." I sighed. This was an old argument that couldn't be won. I sat next to my mother and patted her hand. "Look, I didn't come all this way to fight with you. This is your time. Let's talk about plans for the wedding. I will be happy to help in any way."

And with that, Mary Grace's demeanor changed. I had no silly notions that her meddling would stop, but I was getting a reprieve while she focused on her plans. "I'm so glad to know that, dear, because you're going to be a big part of the ceremony. You and Hugh both, that is. You see, Hugh is going to be the best man, and you're going to be my maid, or rather, son of honor!"

"What? You can't be serious."

"I would never jest about this." Mary Grace sniffed haughtily.

"Why in the world wouldn't you ask Anne Louise? She's been your best friend for years."

"And I've known you your entire life. Please do this for me, Benson. It would mean the world to me. Is it so difficult for you to believe that I would want my only child at my side on such a special day?"

And how in the hell could I argue with that statement?

I couldn't.

A HOT shower wasn't enough to calm me down. I was too keyed up for sleep and decided to take a walk through the grove that marked the end of Winthrop property. The Bayard property began on the other side of the trees. For decades, the Winthrops and the Bayards had been neighbors, the two families united in physical proximity, as well as in purpose and outlook. I'd always considered the grove between the two estates as a sort of no-man's land, belonging to neither of the families. It had often been my refuge. A place I could come to, to be away from the combined demands of the Winthrops and Bayards.

"Hello, Benny."

Startled, I spun around to find Hugh on the other side of the trees. "Jesus Christ, Hugh, would you stop sneaking up on me!"

He walked toward me, and dammit, I wasn't sure if my pulse was racing from being startled or anticipation. "I didn't mean to scare you. It's not like I was trying to be quiet. Besides, I was hoping you would be here."

"Why?" And why did my belly flip-flop? And goddamn it, why did it excite me to no end that Hugh wanted to see me? I had thought I'd put those ridiculous feelings behind me.

"Just wanted to see how things went with your mother."

I frowned. "I suppose you already know she has given me the absurd title of 'son of honor.' I swear."

"I think it was sweet of her."

"And I suppose you think being named best man is sweet too?"

"I'm honored. It means a lot to me that she included me in her wedding."

"Yeah, well, good for you. If I had half a brain, I'd refuse."

"So, tell her you don't want to do it," Hugh said.

"She's my mother. Do you know the hell I'll go through if I told her no? Besides, I tried. She laid the guilt card."

Hugh nodded. That damn teasing smile grew. "Looks like we'll be seeing a lot of each other, then."

I ran my hands through my hair and tucked the longish strands behind my ears. I needed a haircut. I'd never been a fan of long hair on a man, but between work, acting classes, and auditions, I hadn't had time, nor the funds, to be hitting the salon. Then again, I supposed it didn't matter how I wore my hair. Mother had always looked at me as someone frail who needed to be taken care of because of my smaller stature. She still didn't get the concept that big things came in small packages, like dynamite. But whatever. I was stuck with the role of son of honor as well as having to deal with Hugh.

"How about we try not to get in each other's way."

"If that's what you want," Hugh said flatly.

"Look, I'm not trying to be a dick. I just think it would be better if we focus on the task at hand, and no more of this coming to look for me. How'd you know I'd be here, anyway?"

For once, Hugh appeared at a loss. He didn't say anything for a moment. When at last he did speak, it surprised me. "I do you know a little, Benny. You come out here whenever you have a lot on your mind, usually after you've had a run-in with your mother." He glanced around the area, a sly smile forming. "Hey, isn't this where I first kissed you?"

"I don't know, is it?" I asked, even though I knew it was. I was shocked that Hugh would remember.

"Come to think of it, I think it was you who kissed me. I was doing my best to convince you I was much too old for you, but you were determined to show me otherwise."

Old memories drifted over me. The way my stomach had tightened and my entire body tingled with that first brush of lips. That first taste of Hugh set me on a path that was nearly impossible to tread. Like an alcoholic, once addicted always addicted, but that didn't mean I had to give in to that need. I'd fallen off the wagon, but that didn't mean I couldn't jump right back on and move forward. "What's up with the stroll down memory lane? How about we leave the past in the past, shall we, hmm?"

Hugh studied me with a look of purpose in his eyes. I refused to back down. I held his gaze with a hard one of my own. I don't know if Hugh misread my resolve or simply ignored it, but the next thing I knew, my back was pressed against a tree. Hugh was standing very close to me now, too close. I should have shoved him or walked away, but I did neither. I stood there, scarcely breathing.

Hugh raised his hand and ran his thumb gently over my bottom lip. "I remember that kiss. You were inexperienced, but your enthusiasm made up for it. I remember wanting more," he said, his voice husky. "You made me wait two years."

Hugh continued his light, seductive caress, and my eyes fluttered closed. Of course, I remembered the first kiss, every kiss and touch and look. I'd been crazy about Hugh. I'd been nineteen years old when Hugh made love to me for the first time. It had been as if I was waiting for that moment all my life. I was so impatient to have him, and Hugh taught me all the secrets of my body well. How could I have known then that Hugh would become like a drug? A seductive, consuming drug. One I was *still* addicted to.

"When I made love to you in New York, it was like the first time, wasn't it, Benny?"

It had been better than the first time, and that was the problem. Our passion had been all the more intense for its familiarity. I needed more from Hugh than physical passion. Far more.

I forced myself to open my eyes and move away. "Don't do this," I told him with an unsteady voice. I cringed at how weak I sounded. I may have craved Hugh's touch, his kiss, his warmth, but that didn't mean I had to give in to the need. Hugh was bad for my sanity. Dammit, I could resist Hugh. I had to. I cleared my throat and, in a stronger voice, said, "I'm not doing this." I meant it. With my resolve once again firmly in place, I turned and walked away.

CHAPTER FOUR

LIGHT FROM chandeliers glittered on the marble floors and gilded mirrors and the brightly painted ceilings and intricately carved wall panels. The Ashbury mansion in Charleston was far grander than the house I'd grown up in. A hundred years ago, a wealthy society matron named Eva Ashbury had thrown lavish parties here in her efforts to outdo other wealthy society matrons. This evening's gathering was an echo of those splendid affairs. The house now belonged to friends of my mother, and they'd spared no expense in celebrating her impending marriage. At one end of the room, a chamber orchestra played. At the other end, tables had been laden with succulent appetizers.

I wandered along the fringes of the party, sipping a glass of champagne and trying to blend into the backdrop. I'd never been a fan of pompous parties or those who have to flaunt their excessive wealth. Besides, I simply wasn't in the mood to socialize. My ill mood couldn't entirely be blamed on the uppity partygoers or the tight suit jacket or strangling tie. No, it was the way Hugh kept looking at me that was really keeping me on edge. I swore I saw a hint of mockery in Hugh's dark eyes, even from a distance. The infuriating thing was, I couldn't help but continue to glance at Hugh, and each time he caught me. The rush of warmth through my body had nothing to do with alcohol and everything to do with the damn sly grin on his face.

My mother came up next to me. "Having a good time, dear?"

"Just wonderful. It's quite the party."

"Yes, it was so good of them to host such a wonderful event for Charles and me. Wonderful indeed."

Mary Grace was her usual immaculate self—hair perfectly waved, makeup expertly applied. With her usual air of superiority, she glanced about the crowded room. I wanted to cringe or laugh or just get the hell out of there. Of course, being the glutton for punishment that I am, I stood there sipping my champagne, wishing time would speed up.

"Ah, there's Hugh," Mother said in a too-innocent voice. "He looks particularly dashing tonight, don't you think, Benson?"

Unfortunately, I agreed. Hugh's masculine, broad-shouldered frame looked especially attractive in the slate-gray jacket he wore. He exuded confidence, and like a moth to a flame, it drew me in. I turned away, not trusting myself any longer.

"Mother, how about we talk about the decorations or the amazing-looking food, anything besides Hugh?"

Mary Grace's expression was one I'd witnessed numerous times, hell, nearly on a daily basis when I was growing up. She wasn't impressed by my behavior but wouldn't make a scene to save her life. "Benson, please try to act appropriately. I was merely going to point out that you should give him a chance. I'm quite certain he wishes reconciliation with you."

Trust Mary Grace to disregard reality completely. Still, I found myself glancing at Hugh again. By now, a few couples were dancing, and Hugh was among them. He was executing a waltz with a striking blonde woman I didn't know. I tried to ignore the green-eyed monster that rose in me, and tried even harder to convince myself it didn't matter who Hugh danced with.

Several friends approached Mary Grace, giving me the opportunity to escape. I went out to the balcony, leaned against the railing, and stared over the landscape. The evening had deepened into night. The noise of the party was subdued here, and I took my first full breath since arriving at the estate.

"You have a habit of running away, Benny."

"Go away," I said without turning around to face Hugh.

Of course, he didn't heed my warning, choosing to crowd my personal space. He took a deep breath. "Beautiful night."

"I guess, and for your information, I'm not running away. I just don't like this type of party. Too many people."

"Too many of the wrong people, you mean," Hugh said, leaning in even closer.

In some ways, Hugh knew me very well. Too well. "I've never really belonged in this world," I said, gesturing to include the ornate mansion and the expansive grounds. "Everything's on such a grandiose scale. I prefer things small and manageable. But you belong in this world, Hugh. You're very comfortable in it."

"And that gives you one more reason to despise me," Hugh said. The light spilling from the ballroom revealed the hard lines of his face.

"I don't despise you. Believe it or not, I've gone on with my life. I haven't spent every minute thinking about you." That wasn't entirely the truth. I'd spent a lot of time over the past year thinking about Hugh, much to my irritation.

Hugh studied me intently. "Tell me about this life of yours in New York City."

I wasn't comfortable talking to Hugh, or anyone in my family for that matter, about my life in New York. It wasn't only that I knew they would dismiss my dreams as absurd and far-fetched. I was a realist. I knew how far-fetched they were. I didn't need a dose of Hugh's cynical realism. But beyond that, New York was mine, and sharing it with them would tarnish it. "I'm happy," I finally said. "That's all you need to know."

"From what I can tell, you've carved out a lonely place for yourself. Is that how you want it? No family around, no friends?"

"Isn't it wonderful that my life has changed so little when it comes to that aspect?"

"That's unfair."

"But no less true." I took a deep breath to calm myself, but it was no use.

"It wasn't just about my working too much. You always behaved as if you were jealous of anyone or anything that took me away from you."

A twinge of guilt churned my gut. Hugh was right, I had been jealous, but dammit, I had good reason. "Maybe if you'd really been in love with me, maybe then I wouldn't have had to feel that way."

"Your idea of love is completely unrealistic. You expected us to be enthralled with each other twenty-four hours a day. Fairy tales are great when you're curled up with your books, but this is the real world, Ben. I'm just a man, not Prince Charming." Hugh sounded impatient. This was fine with me, considering I was impatient for this conversation to be over.

"Well put," I said snidely. "Except that I'm no longer asking you to be enthralled. You're free."

"It's not as simple as that." Hugh turned and wrapped his arms around me, pulling me close.

I placed my hands against his chest and shoved him away. "Stop it. I'm not doing this."

"What's the matter, Benny? Afraid to admit that at least one thing had been right between us?" He raked his eyes up and down my body with an appreciative gaze. "Very right."

Hugh's touch was dangerous. I knew what that look meant. It had seduced me several times throughout the years. But I was resolute. I would not allow Hugh to crumble me.

"It's not enough. If I wanted nothing but sex, I could pick up any Tom, Dick, or Harry any given night and they wouldn't ask me so many damn questions."

"I won't ask you a single one tonight," he whispered. He stepped up close again. He ran the back of his knuckles gently along my jaw. One touch, that's all it took, and I suddenly had the overwhelming urge to press closer. All rational thought fled me. Hugh began to sway, and as naturally as breathing, I followed. I slid my hands over his shoulders and rose to meet his lips as if I possessed no will of my own.

The spark ignited, and heat rushed through me. My skin tingled as if an electric current were arching between us. I knew I had to do something to break the spell that Hugh had cast over me, but I was powerless. God, how I'd missed dancing with Hugh. How many times had we gone back to each other before the demands of life pulled us apart? No, before Hugh not having time for me pushed us apart. The realization was enough to break the spell, and I ended the kiss.

I pulled away, needing to get some distance and to go search for my backbone. Instead I turned to find my mother watching me from the other end of the balcony. Even from this distance, I could see the satisfied glint in her eyes. I had no clue how long she'd been watching us, but obviously long enough, because she was beaming.

Dammit. Nothing like giving fuel to her pursuits. Still, I wasn't complaining at that moment, because Mother had handed me my spine, and I walked away from both of them without a look back.

CHAPTER FIVE

As I stood under the midday sun, the garden of the Ashbury Estate stirred up some unwanted memories in me. I didn't want to be there—too many conflicting emotions. No matter how lovely the surroundings, this was the same garden where generations of Winthrops had said their vows, me included. Ten years ago. It seemed like a lifetime.

Now it was another summer day, the sun shining down through a crystal blue sky. The beauty was lost on me. Tension radiated along my neck and through my shoulders. All I wanted was for mother's wedding rehearsal to be over and done with, but it hadn't even started yet, and that wouldn't happen until the best man arrived. I was always waiting on Hugh for something. To say I love you, to share his heart, to show up. Same ol' song and dance. I couldn't help but wonder if this was to be my fate or would I one day stop waiting.

I rolled my neck, trying to ease some of the tension. It worked for a moment, but then Hugh came strolling through the gate. He looked good—he always looked good. I tried to turn away, but my body refused to obey my mind. I gave up trying to ignore him and watched as he walked with purpose toward me.

Tie casually loosened and shirtsleeves rolled up over strong forearms, he stopped beside me. "Hello, Benny," he said, his gaze intent on me.

"Hello, Hugh."

For a moment, it seemed that would be the extent our conversation. Hugh, however, didn't excuse himself and go off to speak to someone else. That would have been too easy. Instead, he remained beside me, allowing the silence between us to grow heavy and potent before he nodded toward the opposite side of the garden. "Your mother seems upset," he remarked.

I followed the direction of his gaze to where my mother was deep in consultation with a woman I didn't recognize. I had already noticed the subtle lines of strain on my mother's face. Usually Mary Grace appeared so on top of things, an optimistic manager of people and events, but at that moment, she wasn't managing anything, not even her own wedding rehearsal. She just stood there, looking almost… anxious. I couldn't help but worry. Mary Grace simply wasn't the type to succumb to prewedding jitters.

"You're very observant," I said to Hugh. "Most people wouldn't realize anything's wrong with Mother. They'd just think she was being a little restrained."

"We both know that your mother being restrained is enough of an oddity," Hugh said dryly.

I couldn't help but smile at that, and for a moment, Hugh and I seemed to share something, a sort of insider's knowledge, born of our long history together. But then, Hugh spoke again, and the tenuous sense of intimacy vanished.

"Maybe I'm not so observant," he said. "One thing escaped me entirely, the fact that you want to be an actor, Ben."

"How in the hell do you know about that? Wait. Let me guess. Uncle Johnathan?" I really wasn't shocked. Hell, I expected it to happen. I had a habit of letting my guard down around my uncle. I hadn't told him exactly what I was doing, but he was shrewd, resourceful, and at the age of eighty-two, what did he have to occupy his day but keep up with what his family was doing, that and reruns of *Barney Miller*. I wasn't even that upset. I'd just hoped that I'd have a bit more time to establish myself in New York before it happened.

I glanced over to where my great-uncle was sitting next to Hugh's great-uncle on a wooden bench. They'd been friends forever, more like brothers, and they fought like it too. After Walter Bayard's wife passed away six years ago, he moved into the Winthrop home. He and Uncle Johnathan had been arguing like an old married couple since. I had no doubt they cared for each other, and the more they fought, the more convinced I was that they not only loved each other, but loved the constant banter.

As I watched them, the familiar guilt swirled in my gut. I was the last Winthrop; the whole burden of the Winthrop name rested on me, and I had failed to carry it on. Instead, I'd ended my marriage and run off to New York to pursue my own idea of happiness. I'd been reminded several times by Hugh and my family how amazingly selfish I was for running away to New York. Yet my choice had seemed clear. I could either continue being selfish or suffocate. Hugh was the last Bayard, but he still had a chance. The notion added a good dose of jealousy to the guilt.

"Don't be upset with Uncle Johnathan," Hugh said, pulling me from my musings. "He genuinely cares about you, Ben. And Uncle Walter…. Walter isn't very happy with the fact that Johnathan knew something he didn't. I suspect you'll be getting an earful."

Oh, great! Just what I needed. Still, I felt bad because, no matter what, I truly did love my family, including Walter. He'd been part of my family since I could remember, and I cared for him as equally as I did Johnathan. Hell, I cared and worried about my entire family. I desperately wanted everyone to be happy. I just couldn't live with them.

"I appreciate the fact that they care about me, and I care about them. But, for the first time in my life, I'm doing something on my own, without help from my family. Why does it seem like everyone thinks their happiness is more important than mine?"

Hugh actually seemed to be contemplating my words, or maybe he was trying to figure out what to say that would cause the optimal amount of guilt. That thought put me immediately on the defensive and cranked up the tension in me a couple more levels.

"An actor, huh?" Hugh finally asked. He tilted his head and looked at me with a quizzical expression. "I never knew you wanted to be an actor, or is this some new hobby you've picked up to improve your life?"

"It annoys you, doesn't it? Finding out that something about me was outside your control."

"No, I'm seriously curious," Hugh said, sounding sincere.

"I don't know," I said with a shrug. "It's not like I went around all the time wishing I could be an actor. It wasn't until things got bad between us that I started thinking about what I really wanted to do with my life. And that was when those old childhood dreams popped back up, and I thought why not give it a shot." I didn't mention the immense insecurities that assaulted me every day—every minute. I was trying, and that much I was super proud of.

Hugh continued to study me. "Wow, I had no idea. Is that what you're doing to support yourself?"

I wished. "I'm doing okay." I wasn't about to tell him I was working for minimum wage and barely scraping by. He'd more than likely go behind my back, pay my bills, and stock my refrigerator.

"Next you're going to tell me you have a new man in your life."

I'd not had a single date, and that was part of the problem. Maybe if I had, I could have erased the hold Hugh had over me. I looked away. I was thirty-five years old and still hadn't sown my wild oats, so to speak. I was a bigger fool than Hugh and my family thought I was. No wonder Hugh still had such power over me. Problem was, I hadn't met anyone in New York who attracted me the way Hugh did. It was a hopeless circle. I almost laughed thinking about it, even though it wasn't a particularly humorous situation.

"I'm being nosy," Hugh admitted when I didn't answer. "I'll stop. You don't have to tell me anything."

That was a surprise—Hugh backing off before he obtained what he wanted. I glanced at him suspiciously, but it seemed the rehearsal was starting at last.

As son of honor—damn I hated that stupid title—and best man, Hugh and I were obliged to walk down the aisle together. Ten years ago, I had walked down this exact same path.

"Steady," Hugh said, as if reading my thoughts. He placed his hand under my elbow. "You're not the one getting married in two days. No reason to be nervous."

I huffed out a breath and stared straight ahead.

Just then, I heard a beeping noise, as if my agitated pulse had suddenly acquired sound. The noise, however, was coming from

Hugh. He clasped his hand over his pocket, trying to mute the sound of his phone. At least he had the good sense to look embarrassed. He pulled it out and frowned when he studied the display. "Sorry, I have to take this." He walked back down the stone path and out of the garden. The rehearsal came to an awkward halt, and I'd basically just been abandoned while walking down the aisle.

Hugh returned a few moments later. He glanced at me, then at the rest of the wedding party. "I'm very sorry, but there's something of an emergency. Please go on without me. I'll have Ben fill me in on what I miss."

All I could do was stare at him. I saw his expression, the focused intensity that always came to him whenever he spoke about his job. So things hadn't changed over the past year, not at all, it seemed. Hugh couldn't take even a day or two off without Bayard Investments intruding.

CHAPTER SIX

"THE WEDDING is off!" Mary Grace announced dramatically.

I wasn't sure I'd heard correctly. I stared at her. "You're kidding me, right?"

"I would never joke about such things, Benson. There will be no wedding tomorrow." Mother slumped down onto the chaise like she was fainting, hand to her forehead. Christ, she had such a flair for the dramatics. Except I saw a glimpse of genuine distress. Her face seemed drawn, and her mouth had a pinched look. She appeared truly miserable.

I wanted to help but wasn't sure how to go about it. Mother had been snappish all day, more so than usual. I perched on the edge of the chaise longue, not an easy task since the thing was rather narrow. I patted Mary Grace's shoulder in an awkward attempt to comfort her. "Come, come now, Mother. I'm sure whatever trouble you and Charles are having, it can be worked out. If I had to guess, I'd say you were having prewedding jitters." Shocking for Mary Grace.

She glared at me. "I am having no such thing. It has come to light that Charles and I have a very serious issue that cannot be resolved."

"You know, Mother, Charles is a reasonable man. I'm sure if there's a problem, you can talk to him about it and work it out. I'm absolutely convinced of it, in fact."

Mary Grace straightened and frowned. "Well, isn't this just interesting? I seem to remember telling you the same thing before you ran off and left poor Hugh."

I gritted my teeth. Leave it to Mary Grace to use her problems to try and cajole me into doing what she wanted me to do. "Mother, this isn't about me, it's about you and Charles, remember?"

"How do you know my own situation is any different than what you and Hugh suffered?" Mary Grace asked. "You're assuming

Charles and I can work things out when you were so harsh on Hugh you didn't even try. You should have been willing to listen to his side of things."

It was all I could do to stifle my rising anger. Mother had just broken off her engagement, but she wanted to pursue an in-depth analysis of my life. She was persistent if nothing else. "Mother, let's have some coffee. Then maybe we can figure out what to do about—"

"Oh, Hugh, thank goodness you're here," Mary Grace exclaimed, gazing toward the door.

Hugh walked into the room. I hadn't seen him since he'd left the wedding rehearsal and had no idea why he'd had to leave or what he'd been up to. It was annoying to realize how much I'd been thinking about him.

In Hugh's presence, my mother's poor mood changed drastically. There was a glint in her eye that hadn't been there a moment ago. I began to wonder if all the damn drama was nothing more than a ploy to get Hugh and me together.

Hugh's dark gaze held mine for a moment, and he seemed to be appraising me. I may have sat a little straighter, an old habit. Considering I was perched precariously on the ridiculous sofa, I doubt it did anything to make me look any better.

Hugh turned away to speak with Mary Grace. "I came as soon as I could. What's got you so upset?"

The dramatic flair was firmly back in place. "Oh, Hugh, it's just horrible." She patted the other side of the sofa. "Come sit with me and I'll tell you exactly what happened. I know you'll see my point of view. I'm sure of it." She just had to get in her little digs at my expense.

Not happy with her or the situation, I got to my feet. "Please sit here." My tone exuded my irritation. Hell, I didn't even try to hide it. Like a petulant child, I stomped a few paces away, crossed my arms over my chest, and glared at them both. Only, neither of them were paying me a damn bit of attention. Mother was too busy being attentive toward Hugh and completely ignoring her son.

36

"Charles wants to go house hunting," Mary Grace complained with a bit of a whine to her tone. The sound of it set me off.

"Are you frickin' kidding me? You actually called us both here, making it sound like something was seriously wrong, when it was over nothing more than a spat over the number of bathrooms or some other trivial crap?"

Mother's eyes went wide, then just as quickly narrowed. "How can you be so cruel to suggest something so horrible of me?" She laid her hand over her heart. "My own son thinks so little of me."

"Come off it, Mother. It's obviously an attempt on your part to get allies in your corner so you can use it to control Charles like you are always trying to control me."

"Benson—"

Hugh hopped up and stepped between us, blocking my view of the daggers Mother was shooting at me. "Okay, let's everyone take a deep breath." With his back to me, Hugh addressed her first. "Why does the fact that Charles wants to go house hunting upset you?"

"Because we *have* a house." Mary Grace gestured with her hand around the room. "This house, yet he flat out refuses to live here once we are married. He claims he wants to live in *our* home. Some silly notion that we need something fresh and new, whatever that means."

I was totally on Charles's side. I knew what it felt like to be at a disadvantage. Hugh had chosen the house on Martha's Vineyard and the one in Charleston for himself well before I decided to live with him. At the time, I hadn't questioned moving in, but gradually I'd come to realize that I lived in two luxurious homes that weren't mine. I would have gladly traded both for one small house Hugh and I chose together. Hugh, of course, dismissed any such suggestion. It would be inefficient, unnecessary. And for too long, I had given in. It had been a mistake.

"Mother," I said, stepping around Hugh. "I didn't mean to be insensitive. I shouldn't have snapped at you, but I have to admit, I agree with Charles on this one. What's so horrible about wanting to start your marriage, a new beginning, in a new place? One that belongs to the both of you?"

Mother went rigid, then ignored me. "Hugh, surely you see my side of it. I can't possibly move out and leave the uncles here alone. They need me. With Benson away in New York—" She paused dramatically, making a point to purse her lips at me. "—I'm the only family Johnathan has. And there's certainly room enough in this place for all of us, Charles included."

Hugh shrugged. "Sorry, Mary Grace, but I agree with Ben. As for our uncles, I believe they'll get along just fine here on their own. They're both in remarkably good health, and you already have a live-in housekeeper who can watch out for them. Ben has the right idea. Start fresh with Charles."

I gawked at Hugh. Was he actually agreeing with me about something?

Mother stood up, moved away from the sofa, and in a pained voice said, "Hugh, I can't possibly leave this house. There are so many memories here. This place holds my entire life. I can't walk away from that." Mary Grace looked at me with pleading eyes. "And you, Benson, don't you understand that this is the house where I raised you, where your father and I raised you. Where we first fell in love with you, nurtured you."

I did feel a twinge of sympathy for her. I knew my mother was sincere in her love for my father. She'd been devastated when he'd died of a heart attack. Even though I was only twelve at the time, I vividly remembered her grief. But when it came to the part about raising and nurturing me, she was severely exaggerating. She'd done her duty, given my father an heir. The round-the-clock feeding, dirty diapers, and other such things Mother found unpleasant were left to my nannies.

"Mother," I finally said, "no one's asking you to give up your memories. Charles just wants to make some new ones in a new place. Give him at least that."

"I will not give up my home. I won't marry Charles. I won't marry a man who can't understand how I feel." With that, she got up and hurried out of the room.

I started to go after her, but Hugh grabbed my arm. "Let her have some time to herself. She needs to think it over."

I looked at Hugh's hand, then met his gaze. "Well, no one can ever change her mind once she's decided on something. All she wanted from either one of us was confirmation, and we wouldn't give it to her. The big surprise, though, is that you actually agreed with me, Hugh. What gives?"

"I don't see what the surprise is. It's not like I ever purposely disagreed with you. I do have my own opinions."

"They just always conflicted with mine," I muttered.

"What was that?"

"Nothing."

I took in the room around me. Much of the decor in the house dated back to previous generations of Winthrops. Mary Grace herself had changed only a few details here and there, content to let her husband's family set the tone. How could this house be so important to her when she hadn't truly created it?

"Guess I won't have to bring you up to speed on the wedding rehearsal. How did your emergency go?"

"Just a mix-up at the office. I got it under control. But I seriously doubt you care to hear the details. You never liked me to talk about work."

"Hugh, can't we just make a little polite conversation?"

"Okay, let's give it a try. Everything went as well as can be expected when you're dealing with the eccentricities of a mainframe computer. Anyway, I got the system back online. An updated version is being installed as we speak." He tapped a finger against his chin, then snapped them. "Oh, and I took my office manager out to dinner. I believe you met her once or twice—Michelle Patterson."

"I hope you had a good time," I said without sincerity.

Hugh frowned. "It was a fine evening. Just fine."

"I'm happy for you." I was still on automatic, saying words I didn't mean in the least. But Hugh knew me.

"Come off it, Ben. I can guess how I'd feel if you told me you'd gone to dinner with someone else and you'd had a good time. I wouldn't like it."

"So then you're simply telling me about your date to try to irritate me. Which, if you ask me, is so high school-ish. You know what, it doesn't matter. We're not together anymore. You can do whatever you want," I reminded him.

"You're right, I can, and so can you. But tell me this, why hasn't either one of us become seriously involved with someone else?"

I stared at him with exasperation. "What makes you so certain I'm not involved with anyone?"

"If you were seeing someone, you wouldn't have gone to bed with me last week."

Goddammit! Why did Hugh have to keep bringing up my lapse in good sense? "Listen, you can speculate all you like, but it's none of your damn business."

"You're not seeing anyone," Hugh stated with conviction "And for the past year, I've made sure not to become serious about anyone I've met. Why do you think that is?"

So much for polite conversation. I found Hugh's train of thought to be fascinating and perplexing all at once. "It has only been a year," I pointed out acidly. "Give yourself more time. You're bound to meet up with the right man or woman, someone who can give you a home and children. Someone who doesn't mind putting your needs first."

Hugh stepped closer to me, still frowning. I could feel the rhythm of his pulse, a relentless beat to remind me how readily my body could respond to Hugh.

"We weren't good together," I said, in a low voice. "Even more, we weren't good for each other. But somehow, in spite of that, we always had one thing going for us. We were very good in bed."

"It seems we still are," Hugh murmured in a husky, seductive tone.

"Yes, we still are," I admitted reluctantly. "But we need to forget about it and get on with our lives."

"That's your solution? We pretend nothing happened a week ago?"

"Works for me. I plan on returning to New York and not seeing you anymore."

Hugh looked dissatisfied and paced across the room to the piano that no one played anymore. He plunked two fingers down on the keys. "Avoiding each other is not good enough," he muttered. "There has to be a better way. Believe me, I want to get you out of my system. I'd like to go on to something else… someone else."

"Someone like Michelle Patterson," I suggested.

"I'd be a damn fool to take up with Michelle. She works for me, and she's just getting over her own divorce. But someone like her…. Hell, yes, she's probably the kind of person I should be looking for."

I found myself compelled by a perverse curiosity. "You make her sound different than those women who end up with you in the society pages."

Hugh shrugged. "She's very intelligent and comes from a prominent family." He smiled faintly. "Yet she's the type who prefers taco carryout, hockey games, and spending time with her son."

I gritted my teeth. "Congratulations. Sounds like a match made in heaven."

"You're laying it on a little thick, Ben. All I did was take the woman to dinner."

"And you made sure to tell me about it," I countered.

Hugh shrugged, an unapologetic expression on his face "Maybe I thought telling you would serve some obscure purpose."

"Maybe you just wanted me to be jealous. Or maybe you just wanted to make some official announcement that you're looking to replace me. Someone who can win your approval the way I never could. Someone who loves your damn company as much as you do. Someone who will submit to you and your whims. Someone whose whole life is built around your dreams." At last I managed to clamp my mouth shut. I'd said too much, revealed too much. I knew it by the way Hugh came over to me and took both my hands in his.

"That's unfair. I never asked nor wanted you to spend your life trying to please me. I wanted us to build a life together."

"No, Hugh, you didn't want to build our life. You wanted to build *your* life. I was supposed to fall in line and follow your dreams without question. You never asked about my dreams. Never asked what I wanted, what would make me happy."

"It kills me that I couldn't make you happy, but I definitely never wanted you to 'fall in line,' as you put it. Part of the reason I love you is because of how feisty you are." Hugh slid his arm around me and pulled me close.

I raised my gaze slowly to his. "Maybe at one time you did, but oftentimes the things we like about someone when we first meet them become the things we despise as time goes on. I think that's what happened with us."

"There is nothing I hate about you, Benny. I could never despise you." He bent his head toward mine, pausing with our lips inches apart. My mind and heart went to battle, one telling me to stop this, to take a step back and remember why this was a really bad idea; the other aching to feel Hugh's lips against mine, to have his arms around me, his body against mine. I couldn't move, could barely breathe as my heart overpowered my mind.

CHAPTER SEVEN

HUGH RAISED his head and stepped back. He observed me with that disconcerting intensity of his—disconcerting because I never quite knew what lay behind it.

"Come with me tonight, Ben."

I crossed my arms, dismayed to find myself so shaken. Hugh hadn't even kissed me and I was trembling? Christ, I was a basket case. "I don't think that's a good idea."

"Just come with me." Hugh took my hand and brought it to his mouth. He gently kissed my knuckles, holding my gaze. "Please, Benny. Come with me."

I knew I ought to refuse him, but the battle within me was still raging. I didn't know how to give my mind an edge over my heart. When it came to Hugh, my heart always won. Against all my better judgment, I allowed Hugh to lead me out to his car, and soon we drove through the gates and headed out onto the winding ocean road.

"What kind of adventure are you planning?" I asked.

"What makes you so sure I'm taking you on an adventure?"

"Sometimes I think everything you do turns into an adventure." Hugh could turn even the most ordinary of endeavors into something special and memorable, and living away from him was like celebrating the Fourth of July without fireworks. The job got done, but the sparks were missing.

"Why do you look so perturbed, Benny?"

"It's nothing. And I really wish you'd stop calling me that."

Hugh just kept driving without saying a word. As the landscape flew by, I began to suspect where he was taking me. I curled my fingers into the outer seam of my pants, my body tense. Hugh made a turnoff, and I knew for sure.

"Why did you bring me here?" I asked. My voice cracked with the swell of unwanted memories.

I sat gazing out the windshield. All I could do was stare at the beach house where so much of my life with Hugh had taken place—some of it joyful, a lot of it painful. This was the house where I had first made love with Hugh. This was also the house where I'd told him it was over.

It was a cozy sort of place, built of weathered, silvery wood, etched and decorated by the salty air. It reminded me of a cabin I'd seen in the woods in Tennessee, warm and inviting in its primitive charm. Only, the ocean stretched beyond rather than mountains and lakes.

"Why are we here?" I asked him again.

"I'm not sure. It's not something I planned. It was just…." Hugh cut the engine and swung open his door. "We might as well go inside."

"No."

Hugh came around to my side of the car and opened the door. I stayed where I was.

"Can you please just come inside for a moment?"

I closed my eyes briefly and then climbed out to stand beside him. The air was humid, clinging to my skin, and the breeze whipped strands of hair against my forehead. Every bit of common sense told me not to go into the house with Hugh. Hugh turned, climbed the porch steps to unlock the door. After a second or two, I followed, listening to none of the warnings that clamored inside me. It wasn't my past with Hugh I feared; it was the here and now, very much in the present.

Hugh switched on the lights. I stood in the living room, taking in the place. It had been a year, yet it looked as if I'd just stepped out yesterday. Nothing had changed. The rustic leather sofa and love seat I'd discovered at an estate sale dominated the room. The pillows on it I'd made from fabric I'd found at a thrift shop. The shelves I'd built out of reclaimed wood were stacked with my favorite books.

"It looks the same as the last time I was here," I said in surprise. "I would have thought you'd have decorated it to suit your taste."

"Why would I change it? You always made this place seem… cozy. I liked that feeling. I still do."

I didn't answer. The first time I'd been here, the beach house was being used as a weekend getaway. I had fallen in love with the simple charm and envisioned it as more of a home. I'd also naively imagined Hugh and myself strolling together hand in hand through antique and furniture stores, choosing items that would reflect both our tastes. Hugh had never enjoyed such activities. I had ended up decorating the beach house myself. It had been an engrossing, enjoyable pursuit, but when I'd finished with the job, I experienced a letdown. In spite of the imprint I'd left on the place, it hadn't seemed like a shared home. It still felt like his place and I had merely put a bow on.

I turned around and a photograph crammed on the back of a shelf caught my eye: a framed snapshot showing me and Hugh on the sailboat we'd chartered when we'd vacationed on Martha's Vineyard.

I picked up the photo and studied it. Hugh had his arm around me, and we were laughing at something. We both looked happy. And Hugh… Hugh looked stunning, his hair whipping in the breeze across his handsome face.

"Can I offer you something to drink?"

I fumbled with the photo, nearly dropping it. Thankfully I caught it just in time, and I set it back on the shelf, then turned to face Hugh. "No, thank you. The last time I accepted an invite to drink…." I left the statement hanging.

"Relax," Hugh said. "I'm not trying to seduce you. That's not why I brought you."

"Why did you, then?"

Hugh looked reflective. "I don't know. I guess I just wanted to see if you still fit here."

I gave a mirthless laugh. "You make me sound like a piece of the furniture."

"If by that you mean you belong here, then I agree," Hugh murmured.

"I don't." I heard the shakiness in my voice. "Not anymore." I stabbed my thumb over my shoulder. "Why do you still have that? I would have thought you'd have gotten rid of it."

Hugh's brow dipped as he shifted to look in the direction I'd indicated. "Gotten rid of what?"

"That photo of us."

Hugh stepped over to the shelf and picked up the photo. He smiled fondly. "Why would I do that? It's a great picture of us."

"I'd think it would be hard to explain to prospective dates."

Hugh tilted my chin up with one finger and studied me thoughtfully. "You're the only one I've brought home."

I was ridiculously happy that Hugh hadn't shared this place with anyone but me. It was special, our place. At least for the moment. I held Hugh's gaze, my throat dry with emotion, unable to speak.

Hugh kept on touching me and looking at me. He then bent his head and brushed his lips over mine. Once, and then again, Hugh tantalized me with just the briefest touch of his mouth. I closed my eyes, welcoming him.

Hugh brought his arms around me, pulled me close, and deepened the kiss. All the warning bells inside me went off once again. We had to stop now. Only a kiss. If we stopped, it wouldn't be too late. Even as the thoughts were flittering through my mind, I brought my arms around Hugh. I moved even closer to him. I wanted him. I needed to feel him pressed against me, touching me, consequences be damned.

We began to move toward the bedroom, one step at a time. Still kissing, hands roaming, we bumped against the wall. One last warning echoed faintly in my head. *Don't do this. Run!* I didn't listen. I was beyond listening. We made it through the door of the bedroom and onto the bed. Hugh tangled his hands in my hair, and I arched my neck as his warm lips pressed to my throat. A tingling sensation raced down my body. My cock was achingly hard.

I tugged at Hugh shirt, fumbled with buttons, impatient with the fabric that kept Hugh's skin from me. Hugh, obviously aware of my frustration, lifted himself up a little and undid just enough buttons so he could pull the offending garment over his head and throw it behind him. I ran my hands through the dark swirl of hair on his chest, then tweaked each nipple until they were erect.

I leaned up and took one hard nub into my mouth, teased it with tongue and teeth, and pulled a long rumbling moan from Hugh. With a satisfied smile, I gave the other nipple the same treatment. Hugh interrupted the teasing by yanking my shirt off and tossing it to the floor. He winked at me—a challenge I accepted with relish. Frantically, we unzipped our pants and popped the rest of the buttons, clothes and shoes falling away until at last there were no more barriers between us. I wrapped my body around Hugh, begging without words.

Now that we were naked, my body screaming for release, Hugh slowed things down. He refused to hurry. "I want to look at you," he murmured. He reached over to turn on the bedside lamp, and light cascaded over us. He sat back on his calves; his eyes filled with lust as he took in my body. His long thick cock was straining, bobbing with each breath he took. My mouth watered. I wanted to taste him, but I knew Hugh. He would make me wait. This was the one aspect of my life where I willingly gave over complete control.

Hugh leaned down and brushed his cheek across my chest; the dark stubble tickled. I squirmed beneath him. My amused response turned into a moan of approval when Hugh took one stiff nipple into his mouth—a spark of pain as his bit down on the nub. Then he eased the sting with his tongue. As he continued his assault on my chest, he slid his hand down my stomach, grasped my cock, and stroked it with long, firm pulls. He was slow and deliberate in his movements, building the desire within me until the pleasure was so keen it bordered on pain.

"Hugh, please." I clutched his shoulders, thrust my hips.

He wasted no time rolling on a condom. He poured a small amount of lube into his palm then wrapped it around my cock stroking it with slow, gentle pulls, not enough to push me over the edge but to keep me teetering on it. I bit my lip to keep from begging. It would only fuel Hugh to tease me further. He loved to hear me beg knowing I would only do so when I was ready to explode. It had always been his favorite game and, I had to admit, one of mine as well—even if it was beyond maddening.

One slick finger, then two readied my body for him. Hugh pulled his fingers free, then grasped his cock and guided it to my opening. He held my gaze as he slowly entered me. I gasped at the burn, but Hugh kept pushing slowly forward, kept watching me until he was deep within my body. His thrusts started out painstakingly slow, in sharp contrast to my hammering pulse. Sweat bloomed on my flesh. Our bodies easily slid against each other, moving in perfect harmony. The pleasure built to a feverish pitch until I couldn't stand it a second longer.

"So close, please, Hugh," I groaned.

It was the cue Hugh was waiting for. He lifted my legs, nearly bent me in half, pounded into me. "Come for me, Benny."

I arched my back, muscles bowstring tight for a second. One last hard thrust from Hugh and I was shoved over the edge. I clutched at him and pulled him over with me as we both gave in to the demands of our bodies.

Hugh collapsed on top of me. I let my legs fall to the mattress, wrapped my arms around him, and held him as we came down from the high.

Once the passion cooled, I sensed the subtle shift in Hugh as he closed himself off from me. He didn't turn his back on me. He rolled onto his side and lay there next me, one arm draped across my body. But I could sense him shutting down nonetheless. I could see it in the way he seemed to look past me, not directly into my eyes. That was the amazing thing. In the most intimate moments of lovemaking, Hugh often gazed at me, inside me, it seemed. But afterward… afterward, Hugh always gazed *past* me, exactly as he was doing now. It made me feel as if I'd just gone to bed with a stranger.

I tried to slide quietly from the bed, but before my feet were on the floor, Hugh grabbed my arm. "Stay."

I froze. Although the word was a command, I could hear the plea in his voice. It was enough to make me stay. I lay back down, scarcely breathing, daring to hope. Countless nights in this very bed, even with Hugh lying next to me, I'd felt alone. I never knew where he went; I only knew he was no longer with me, even though his physical body was, his mind was far, far away.

Hugh didn't look at me, but he pulled me close. He ran a single finger up and down my arm in a random pattern. He didn't speak, but he knew I was there. He wanted me there. The spark of hope burned a little brighter.

CHAPTER EIGHT

THE MUSTY smell of the theater rose around me. I imagined it as the odor of a thousand shabby dreams. Well, today I'd brought my own slightly shabby dream into this small, decrepit theater. This was the same theater where I'd performed such a rotten audition two weeks ago, reading the part of an eccentric uncle. Yesterday Frank informed me that the role was still open. He'd somehow managed to wrangle a copy of the script for me, and I'd studied it thoroughly. I could tell that this was destined to be a rather rambling and pretentious play, but the role of the uncle did have possibilities. Who was I kidding, anyway? I wanted desperately to act. I didn't care how good or bad the play was, if only I could be in it. So much for my pride. A solid year of rejections had taken care of that.

I walked briskly down the narrow aisle of the theater, confident of my abilities. Three or four people clustered in front of the stage, among them the same red-haired woman.

"Have a seat," she told me with little apparent interest. "I'll get to you in a minute."

I settled back into the chair and took a few deep breaths, then opened the script and flipped through a few of the pages, rereading lines. But I couldn't relax. Too many thoughts kept intruding, of failure, of success… of Charleston.

I'd left Charleston four days ago, and I'd been worried about Mother ever since. It didn't help that every time I called her and began a sensible discussion, she lost her temper and hung up on me. I had been branded a traitor for siding with Charles. It seemed that Mother had broken off all negotiations with her ex-fiancé and was ready to break off all communication with anyone who so much as mentioned his name. From the sound of things, she wasn't spending very much time with her friends. She'd always been like this. If people didn't agree with her, then she simply refused to talk to anyone until they came around to "proper" thinking. She was as stubborn as a mule, and there really was no point in trying to talk to her until she was ready. Totally pointless.

Then there was Hugh. I had thought of little else but him since I'd left the beach house. Whether it had been real, or wishful thinking on my part, I had sensed a change in Hugh. He'd asked me to stay, had held me until I'd fallen asleep. He was trying—or at least I thought he was. Of course, in the morning, Hugh was all business, emotionally closed off as he rushed me home so he could get to the office. Here in the dimness of the theater, my face burned with anger at the memory of going to bed with that bastard again. The first time, I'd had an excuse: excessive alcohol. The second time, I had no excuse at all.

In annoyance I tapped the script against my knee. One mistake I could forgive myself. Two mistakes I couldn't. I despised my weakness.

"Of course, you could just sit there," Red said. She waved a flippant hand. "Fine with me."

I scrambled to my feet. I couldn't believe I'd been so distracted I hadn't heard the summons to the stage. I'd allowed thoughts of Hugh ruin my last audition, and I'd be damned if I'd allow him to ruin this one as well. I walked briskly down the aisle and up the steps.

Red glared at me for a moment, then sighed dramatically. "I suppose you might as well read with Jason."

A man of about twenty-five climbed onto the stage beside me, carrying a copy of the script. My stomach tightened from nerves, but I managed to give him a brief professional nod. Quickly I thought about the character I was supposed to play—a man slipping off the edge of middle age, hiding his nature and his passion beneath a cloak of indifference. I clenched the script and took another deep breath. The first line was mine, and I began speaking the words, rushing them. Emotion—where was the emotion I should feel? Dammit, I wasn't Ben Winthrop anymore. I was a man named Edgar, speaking to a young man half his age who had ignited forbidden desires and hid them behind a facade of anger. Except, I didn't feel anger, or any other emotion appropriate to the character. I just felt awkward and ridiculous, and I was reading too fast.

"Start again," interrupted Red, sounding impatient.

I couldn't believe I'd already bungled things. My throat had gone dry, my chest was constricted, and my damn palms were sweating.

"You'll do fine," Jason whispered. "Remember, it's just a part."

I glanced at him. Jason was pleasant-looking, with fair coloring and hazel eyes. And somehow he'd managed to say just the right thing. He made me realize I was taking this part too seriously. I had to play around with it a little. I had to think of it as trying on a new suit, not as wearing a straitjacket.

I took one last deep breath, then tried again. The lines flowed easily this time. "I have no time for you. Be gone."

"What do you mean you have no time for me? You asked me to come."

I kept trying to relax. It was a short scene, but it was also one of the best in the play, where the uncle comes to realize how scared he is and dismays over his lack of control.

I took a turn around a small crate littered with shredded newspaper. The stage directions read "Edgar walks to the mantel, keeping his back to his niece's boyfriend." I tried to improvise. "I made a mistake."

"Why are you so cold—"

I spun and glared at Jason. "I said—"

"Okay, okay," Red interrupted. "No need to drag it out. Thank you, Mr.… Whatever."

I lowered the script. It took me a second or two to let go of Edgar. The audition was already over. Usually that made me feel relieved. Today I just felt a peculiar sense of loss. I hadn't even gotten started and I was being shooed away.

The red-haired woman, however, was already speaking to someone else. I turned to Jason. "Thanks," I said.

"Hey, no sweat, you did great."

I wasn't sure at all how I'd done. Obviously, Red wasn't impressed. But anyway, the session was over. I went down the stage steps and walked back up the aisle. I moved automatically, a sharp disappointment going through me. One more audition, one less part to play. It didn't make for the most balanced equation.

"Be here at seven tomorrow."

I twisted around and gawked at the red-haired woman, who was still looking bored. "You want me to read again?"

"I want you to know the damn lines."

For a long minute, I didn't understand. "Do you mean—"

"You want Edgar or not?"

Still not daring to believe it, I wished she would just come out and say it. Well, if she wouldn't, I would. "I got the part?"

She looked resigned. "You got the part. That is, unless you have issues with kissing another man?"

Actually, I prefer it. I swallowed down a snort of laughter. "No, ma'am."

"Seven o'clock tomorrow night, then."

I didn't know how I made my way from the theater, but a few moments later, I was standing on the sidewalk outside. Everything looked wonderful to me—the boarded-up storefront across the street, the garbage clotting the gutter, the grimy marquee of the theater itself. I had a part. *I actually have a part! A role to play.* I felt like screaming. I felt like calling up Hugh and telling him the fantastic, stupendous, incredible news.

This impulse brought me up short. I stood there in front of the seedy little theater. Why would I want to call my ex, of all people? What was wrong with me?

Surely, Hugh was the last person who'd understand why I was so happy at this moment. And that marred my happiness.

Would I never be free of Hugh Bayard?

"Congratulations," said a voice beside me.

Absorbed in my own thoughts, I hadn't noticed Jason come out of the theater.

I smiled. "Listen, thanks for what you did in there. You helped me relax and get through it."

He stuck out his hand to shake mine. "Jason Collins, alias Pete, alias partner in the Stewart Mott Playhouse. A pretty grandiose name for this dump of ours, but someday I'll have to tell you all about Stewart, our eccentric founder. He deserves a little grandiosity."

So, Jason Collins was not only an actor. "Well… thanks again," I said.

"Aren't you going to tell me your name? Technically I'm your new boss, although Joyce Draper likes to think she's the one calling the shots."

Joyce Draper was no doubt the red-haired woman. I felt as if I'd just plunged into an intriguing new world. I was now officially one of the Stewart Mott players. I liked the sound of it. A little grandiosity was fine with me.

"I'm Ben Winthrop. It's been nice meeting you, Jason, and I'll see you tomorrow night at seven—"

"Let me buy you a cup of coffee to celebrate."

I wanted to share this moment of excitement with someone. Foolishly I still wanted that someone to be Hugh, but he wasn't here. He wasn't part of this new life of mine. That was the way it had to be.

"A cup of coffee sounds great."

We walked a few blocks to a small Italian restaurant and slid into a booth, facing each other. We ended up not only with coffee but also with servings of amoretti cake.

It was delicious, but it could have been sawdust and I would have eaten it gladly. I felt benevolent toward everything and everyone. I wanted to order amoretti cake for the entire place, except Jason and I were the only ones there. No matter. This moment was what I had longed for. I repeated it over and over in my mind. I had a part. I had a role. I was Edgar.

Jason propped his elbows on the table. "Tell me what you're thinking. I can't decide whether you look like someone who just got hit by a bus or someone who just won the lottery."

"I feel a little of both," I admitted. "This is my first break. My first acting role."

"Don't get carried away," he warned. "The pay's rotten, and we'll be lucky if we get an audience."

"I don't care. I'll always remember this moment. Where I was, what I was doing." I glanced around so I could set these surroundings into my memory. My gaze came back to rest on Jason, and I realized how crazy I sounded. "I'm not usually like this. I'm usually very calm."

Jason smiled. "Hey, I'm just glad I could be here to share the moment. You're not jaded yet. I like that."

Jason had a nice smile. His hair was sandy colored and grown long enough to curl over his collar, and he had a slightly ruddy complexion as if he'd spent time out in the sun. He was quite handsome.

"I'm jaded about enough things," I admitted. "It comes with age. I'm thirty-five, after all."

"Interesting," Jason remarked, "the way you're already setting up barriers. Very well. I'm twenty-six. Not all that different from thirty-five."

Was I really setting up a barrier? Perhaps. It took me a moment to sort it out. I'd felt a little attracted to a man other than Hugh, and then I'd felt oddly guilty about it. Christ, I was behaving as if I'd been disloyal to my ex. How ridiculous. We were through. Finished! No matter that I'd slept with him again.

I poured extra sugar into my coffee. "I'm just getting into character. I'm supposed to play the older man, aren't I?"

Jason stirred his coffee slowly. "Tell me a little about yourself. I'm curious. You say this is your first role. But you must have acted in college or high school. All of us have stories about our tenth-grade drama teachers."

"I might as well admit it. I was always too much of a coward to try out for high school or college plays. I had this dream about being an actor, but it was never anything more than that. After college, well, life got in the way."

"Something tells me you're making up for lost time," Jason said.

"That's one way to put it." All my years with Hugh—could I call it lost time? In too many ways, I had lost myself in him. I couldn't deny that, but it wasn't something I wanted to talk about.

"You seem to be doing pretty well," I said to Jason. "You're already co-owner of a theater and you're only twenty-six."

"I've just sunk all my money into a rundown theater in a shady part of the city—maybe I'm crazy, maybe I'm smart. Too soon to tell." He cocked his head. "So, how do you feel about playing an older gay man?"

"I've been doing it all my life, well, not the old part." I chuckled, nervously watching Jason for his reaction. It was one thing to play a gay man, completely different story to be one. At least to some people.

Jason sat back with a satisfied smile. "Well, Ben Winthrop, you have just made my night." With the way Jason was looking at me appreciatively, there was no question as to his sexual preference.

I smiled and my stomach fluttered. Perhaps the excitement of getting my first part was messing with me. I ignored the strange feeling Jason brought out in me. "Then that makes two of us having great nights." Suddenly uncomfortable with where the conversation was heading, I slid from the booth and stood. "Look, thank you for celebrating with me, Jason. But I have to get back to work."

Jason rose. "Will you have dinner with me tonight?"

"You don't waste any time, do you."

"Not when it counts," Jason said. "So, what do you say? I'll pick you up at eight."

I hesitated, then shook my head. "It's not such a good idea."

"Let me guess, those nine years again?"

"No, that's not it. I'm… sort of involved with someone right now," I lied, then wanted to kick myself. What was wrong with me? A handsome, younger man was inviting me to dinner, and I had to invent excuses?

"Sort of involved," Jason echoed. "Do tell."

"It's difficult to explain." I wished I hadn't even started. "It's just… complicated."

Jason looked disappointed. "You know you're in trouble when a man tells you it's complicated. The *C* word. Bad news all around."

I couldn't help smiling again. Jason really was engaging. I put out my hand to shake his. "I'll see you tomorrow at the theater."

Jason smiled warmly. "Tomorrow it is."

We parted at the door of the restaurant, and I felt a tinge of regret. I had a suspicion I was going to like working with Jason, so why hadn't I accepted his invitation? Such a simple, ordinary thing, going out to dinner with someone. Why couldn't I just let it be simple and ordinary? Why had I fabricated that nonsense about being involved? Showing poor judgment and going to bed with an ex did not constitute involvement. Even if I'd done it twice.

"Damn you, Hugh Bayard," I grumbled, then rushed back to work.

The crowd at the Common Cure made it difficult to get through the door, but knowing I was going to have another crazy shift couldn't put a damper on my mood. The smile on my face as I pushed through toward the back was so big, it nearly split my face. I had a part!

In the kitchen, Geovanni was screaming, the cooks scrambling. I scanned the room until I found the familiar ponytail. I snatched my apron off the hook and put it on as I made my way to Mel.

She looked relieved when she spotted me. "Oh, thank God. The salad bar is demolished." She cocked her head, a smile forming. "Wait! From the look on your face…." She grabbed my arms and started jumping up and down. "You got the part!"

"I got the part!" I confirmed.

We bounced up and down like fools. It felt so good to have someone as excited about my accomplishment as I was.

"I knew you would do it. This is so frickin' awesome!" Mel threw her arms around me and hugged me. "Just make sure you remember the little people when you're a famous actor."

"It's a small part in a rundown theater. I doubt I'll be hitting the big screen or Broadway anytime soon." I chuckled.

"And you won't be getting a paycheck anytime soon if you don't get to work!"

Mel jerked back, her eyes wide, showing the same shock I felt. How in the hell had Geovanni overheard us with the noise level in the kitchen? The surprise quickly wore off. Mel pecked my cheek. "Congrats."

"Thanks." I winked and hurried to off to refill the salad bar. I was officially an actor. Holy shit—an actor. I wanted to scream it to the world. But that would have to wait until the lunch crowd was satisfied, unless I wanted to be a *homeless* actor.

CHAPTER NINE

FOR WHAT seemed the hundredth time, I repeated the opening to act 3, scene 5.

"Why must you bother me? I simply—"

"Wrong, Winthrop," snapped Joyce for what also seemed the hundredth time. "All wrong. I told you to be nasty. Sour. Insincere. Got it?"

I shifted in my chair, my muscles cramped from sitting so long. The theater had no air-conditioning, and I was sticky with perspiration. "I'm sorry. I'm having a hard time making Edgar such a sarcastic and underhanded person," I said with as much patience as I could muster. "Edgar genuinely cares for his niece. I feel sorry for him. He's so tortured by what he's feeling for her boyfriend."

"Oh, wonderful. The sensitive routine." Joyce pushed lank strands of that improbable red hair away from her face. "Just give Edgar some backbone, will you?"

"Of course he has backbone. Of course he's going to do the right thing in the end. But does he have to be so damn nasty?"

"Winthrop, I don't want a dissertation. Just say the lines, and say them the way I tell you."

I clenched my hands. All week Joyce and I had been working up to this disagreement. Joyce wanted me to portray the character as lonely, embittered, and spiteful. I saw Edgar as lonely, impassioned, and confused. Every instinct in me told me I was right about this. Edgar needed to be seen as a character with redeemable qualities. I wasn't winning any popularity contests with Joyce.

Jason leaned forward in his chair. "I think we should listen to Ben. The role of Edgar is pivotal. If his tone is off, the relationship between Edgar and Pete will be off too."

Joyce glared at Jason. "We agreed that I'm the director on this one. At least, that's what I thought we agreed."

Lindsey, the nineteen-year-old playing the niece, slapped her script shut. Everything about Lindsey seemed pared down—she was slight in build, her hair cropped short, her nails always nibbled to the quick. Put her on a stage, though, and she became bigger than life. She sparkled, a small gem suddenly magnified. She was a very good actress, and she'd given me a few pangs of envy already.

"Excuse me, everybody," Lindsey said. "But all we've done the whole night is argue about Edgar, Edgar, Edgar. Can we just get on with it?"

"No," said Joyce. "We're done for tonight. Winthrop, when you show up tomorrow, be ready to do it my way." With that, she left the stage, moving with her usual world-weary air.

Lindsey, after a resentful glance at me, stalked off too. Only Jason and I remained. The lights glared down on us as if they were as irritated as Lindsey and Joyce. I sighed and reached up to massage the sore muscles in my neck. "I didn't imagine it would be like this," I said. "I pictured camaraderie, teamwork. Except that I just can't keep my big mouth shut, but I really think Joyce is wrong on this. I've begun to think of Edgar as a real person. I know him and I have to defend him."

"For what it's worth, you're right. This play is going to be hard enough to sell as it is. If the audience can't identify with Edgar, we'll really be in trouble."

"I'm probably opening my mouth again when I shouldn't, but… I don't quite understand the hierarchy. You and Joyce."

"It's your basic power struggle," Jason said ruefully. "Joyce has really had a hard time of it just trying to keep this theater company going. She resents like hell taking me on as an investor, even though she needs me. She doesn't like sharing her authority yet. She'll just have to get used to it, though. I plan to make some big changes." He smiled wryly. "Besides, after she came on to me and I had to inform her she had the wrong plumbing, it sort of put a damper on her good feelings for me."

"She came on to you? Wow, I wouldn't have thought…."

"What? You don't think I'm attractive enough that a woman would want to hit on me?"

"I didn't mean that at all," I said quickly. Jason wasn't ruggedly good-looking, but he was handsome in a cute sort of way. "I only meant that she has to be what? Twice your age?"

"Age is just a number, and it would be good for you and for me to remember that." Jason winked at me, then stood and came around to massage my shoulders. "Wow, you really are tense. You need to loosen up."

I groaned as Jason's thumbs pushed on a particularly painful knot. "Arguing with Joyce all night is stressful."

"I'm sorry, but honestly, I'm glad you're standing up to her and fighting for what you think is right. I have faith that you'll make Edgar a real and unforgettable character."

"Thanks." Jason's praise and his talented fingers allowed me to let go of some of the tension. I relaxed back against the chair, took deep calming breaths, and felt the stress seep slowly from me.

"Are you hungry? We could grab something at that little diner I've been trying to get you to try."

"Depends on your intentions," I said.

"My intentions are filling my stomach with great food and enjoying your company," Jason explained.

I slipped out of my chair and turned to face him. "And that's it?"

"Yes," he insisted. "You know I want to get to know you better, but I also know your life is complicated, you think you're too old for me, and there's some guy you're involved with, sort of. Did I cover everything?"

"Pretty much," I agreed.

"Good, then how about two actors go enjoy a great pastrami sandwich as a reward for our hard work. My treat."

Every evening this week after rehearsal, Jason had asked me to dinner. And every evening I'd given him the same answer—no. Either it was his new approach or he was wearing me down because I couldn't think of a single reason not to accept his offer. More importantly, I wanted to accept it. I was starved and pastrami sounded a lot better than the frozen dinner waiting for me at home.

"All right, lead the way."

"Great!" Jason beamed.

I stuffed the script into my messenger bag, then went down the stage steps, Jason right next to me. We walked all the way to the door, but then I turned and glanced back. It really was a decrepit theater, with its tattered seats and faded curtains, but it still seemed special to me, a place for magic.

"Gets to a person, doesn't it?" Jason murmured as if reading my thoughts. "Even when I was a kid, I was fascinated by the contrast, the stage all lit up, the darkened theater. I'd sit in the audience and it felt to me like those people on the stage were in a different land. A land where I longed to be."

"That's exactly how I felt as a child," I admitted. "I always thought once you stepped onto that stage, it was like going through an invisible door into another world."

We stood together for a moment, sharing a quiet companionship. It was a pleasant feeling, soothing after the rehearsal I'd just endured. I allowed the moment to draw out a bit, and then I left the theater with Jason.

Night had fallen, but the air still seemed close. It pressed in on me with all the grime and soot of the day. I said a small prayer for the wind to blow hard enough to chase away the heat and the dirt.

A black limousine pulled up at the curb. It was a vehicle I knew altogether too well, and it looked completely out of place on this squalid street. Nonetheless, a tinted window slid down and a familiar face peered out. My mother.

"Benson, there you are, sweetheart! I've found you at last." Mary Grace smiled fondly, apparently forgetting that only last night she'd slammed the phone down in my ear yet again.

I stepped closer to the car. "Mother, how did you find me?"

Mary Grace leaned out the window. "Uncle Johnathan is having a wonderful time reviving his connections with the theater. He's the one who managed to track you down, dear. Very enterprising of him, I must say. Aren't you going to introduce me to this nice young man?"

Jason had stepped up to the limo beside me, and he held out his hand to Mary Grace. "Jason Collins. So you're Ben's mother. It's a pleasure to meet you."

"How charming," Mary Grace cooed.

"Ben and I were just heading down to get something to eat. Perhaps you'd like to join us, Mrs. Winthrop?"

"I don't think—" I began.

"Oh, if you're sure it won't be an imposition," Mary Grace exclaimed, still poking her head out the window of the limousine.

"Of course not," Jason said, portraying the very image of geniality. "Ben and I would be delighted to have your company, wouldn't we, Ben?"

Mary Grace swiveled her perfectly groomed head and gazed expectantly at me. What a pair. Jason and Mary Grace had known each other only seconds, but already they were a team. It was highly irritating.

I grimaced, but I didn't see that I had much choice in the matter. I was still worried about how Mother was handling her broken engagement, and now that she was right here, I had to take advantage of the opportunity to check up on her. Of course, at the same time, I had to tolerate my mother checking up on me. What a mess!

"Very well, Mother. Let's all have dinner together."

"Wonderful," Mary Grace said in a tone of satisfaction. As if on cue, her stiff-faced chauffeur came around to swing open the door of the limousine.

"Good evening, Mr. Winthrop," he said to me in very correct tones.

"Good evening, Vance. How are you?"

"Quite well, Mr. Winthrop."

It was a superficial exchange. Mary Grace surrounded herself by only the most stern and off-putting of employees—people who took their jobs much too seriously in my opinion. While I was growing up, all my nannies had been like that, very serious, very correct.

I climbed into the limo and was followed by Jason. The blessedly cool air of the vehicle immediately engulfed me. That was one thing about wealth—it was very helpful in matters of climate control.

A moment later the car purred away from the curb, riding as smoothly as if the shocks were cushioned in silk. That was another thing about wealth—its cushioning effect. I found it exasperating, but at the same time, I couldn't help sinking back into the comfort of leather upholstery.

Jason and I sat opposite Mary Grace like two subjects summoned before the queen.

"How delightful this is," Mary Grace said. "Now, you must allow me to be something of a bore and take you to Deluca's, my favorite restaurant. My treat, of course."

I winced, for Mary Grace was referring to one of the most exclusive establishments in the entire city.

"Mother, we had plans. Jason assured me the pastrami at the local diner is delicious, and I am really looking forward to trying it."

Mary Grace wrinkled her nose. "You know I don't like pastrami. Besides, dear. I really am a fuddy-duddy, I'm afraid. Deluca's is the only place I can possibly eat when I'm in New York. You don't mind, do you, Jason?"

"No, of course not. Although, I'm really not dressed for anything upscale," Jason said.

For a brief second, I thought I was going to get a reprieve. But of course, I was delusional. Mary Grace waived a dismissive hand. "Nonsense. I have set up for private dining, as I so much wanted to get caught up with what my son has been up to. All those prying eyes and hearing aids set on high. You're absolutely presentable." I gritted my teeth. Leave it to Mother to dash my dreams.

Only a short time later, I left the buffered interior of the limo for the equally buffered interior of Deluca's. I couldn't help but wonder what Mary Grace was up to. The woman never did anything without some ulterior motive. I sat across from her at the table and looked her over carefully. Something about her seemed awry. Maybe she was simply too cheery for someone who'd broken off her engagement on the eve of the wedding.

"Now, Jason, I highly recommend the lobster frittata," Mary Grace said as Jason settled himself between mother and son. "Of course, there is always the calamari, but I've never been very adventurous. What do you think?"

"Lobster frittata it is," Jason announced. "So, Mrs. Winthrop, I'd love to hear more about Ben. He's much too secretive a person."

"Please, call me Mary Grace, and I agree with you. Ben most certainly is secretive. If his uncle Johnathan hadn't found him out, none of us would know about his acting career. A shame because we're all proud of Benson. Even Hugh, of course."

"Hugh?" Jason asked.

Dammit, here we go, I thought. Irritation crept along my nerve endings. I folded my arms over my chest and sat rigidly. I wasn't having the least bit of fun. Suddenly the isolation of my drab little apartment and a frozen dinner sounded like heaven on earth.

Mary Grace leaned toward him confidentially. "Benson's ex-husband. Surely you know about Hugh?"

"Afraid not," Jason said, regarding me now.

"Oh, dear, I've put my foot in it." Mary Grace looked pleased. She didn't say anything more, allowing Hugh's name to linger evocatively in the air.

I refused to let Mother's manipulative tactics get the better of me. I perused the menu with great deliberation.

It was Jason who finally broke the charged silence. "I've never been married," he remarked. "Did I tell you that, Ben?"

"Yes, I believe you did."

"Thought so. Sometimes those little details between two people can be important," Jason pointed out.

I glanced over the top of the menu. "Jason, I've only known you a week."

"Sometimes a week is all it takes," he said seriously, addressing Mary Grace. "I like Ben. I wish I could get to know him better. But he didn't even tell me that he has an ex lurking in the wings."

"In the wings? My, I like that. You really are an actor. But Benson hasn't always been so reticent," Mary Grace went on. "It's only been this past year, since he left Hugh. That's really the way it was, you know. He left Hugh. It's all quite a puzzle."

"I'll say." Jason paused. I couldn't tell if he was really thinking or doing it for flare. He was an actor, after all. "With Ben, it's one puzzle after another. For instance, he keeps being mysterious and telling me he's involved with someone, but I never see him around."

"Goodness," said Mary Grace, looking concerned. "A mystery man. I hadn't counted on that."

I closed the menu and curled my hands into fists. What I really wanted to do was throttle both my dinner companions. "This conversation is mesmerizing, but I'd like to change the subject—"

"Benson, who on earth are you involved with?" Mary Grace persisted. "Who is this mystery man?"

"Wouldn't we all like to know," Jason put in.

The two of them stared at me. I stared back unflinchingly, purposefully keeping my features neutral. A herculean effort considering what I really wanted to do was get my ass up and walk out. Instead I sat there with the two of them acting like inquisitors. Well, they could question me all they wanted. I wasn't about to confess that my ex and the so-called mystery man were one and the same. It would be mortifying, particularly as I wasn't involved with Hugh. I had made a mistake—two mistakes—that was all.

I picked up the menu again. "I'm ready to order."

Mary Grace stared hard at me but then retreated behind her own menu. "I really do hope you're going to have the lobster, Benson."

"Nope. I'm going for the chicken terrine." I knew it didn't matter what I ordered. I doubted that anything would sit well on my stomach.

Jason and Mary Grace behaved themselves reasonably well throughout dinner. The two of them chatted like old friends, but that was a problem. Mary Grace had so easily intruded on my new life, and Jason seemed to be having a grand time. Apparently, I was the only one who wasn't.

At last, the meal was over. I hadn't eaten much; the nervous rumbling in my gut wouldn't allow it. But no matter, I had a half gallon of ice cream with my name all over it at home. Ice cream at night, like coffee in the morning, made the world bearable. I pushed my chair back with relief, but Jason and Mary Grace prolonged matters.

They pursued an involved discussion over who should pay. Finally, I snatched the bill, cringed when I saw the amount, and handed it to Mary Grace.

"Mother, thank you. Jason, you'll just have to display your masculine pride some other way. And now we're going!"

They didn't argue with me. Thank God. We rode to Jason's apartment in complete silence. Which was a huge relief because I wasn't sure how much more I could take. I was tired, cranky, and just over it.

"Mrs. Winthrop, this has been a most pleasant evening," Jason said solemnly.

Mother beamed. "I should hope so. You really are a very nice young man, but it appears that you have a great deal of competition where Benson is concerned. Not only do you have the mystery person to deal with, but I warn you that Benson's ex is not completely out of the picture."

"I've always enjoyed competition—"

Oh, for the love of God. I'd had enough fun for one night. "Good night, Jason," I said, not even trying to hide my irritation.

Jason hesitated, looking at me with a questioning expression. I glared at him, leaving no doubt as to how serious I was. Finally, Jason stepped out of the limo, and it glided forward again.

I sank back against the leather cushions. "All right, Mother," I said with as much self-control as I could muster. "I know what you're trying to do. You're trying to avoid your own problems with Charles by poking your nose into my life."

"Forget Charles. Charles is history. I can't believe how busy you've been, Benson. That nice young Jason is besotted with you, and you have the mystery man as well. Tell me who he is. I simply must know."

A strangled snort of laughter escaped me. The whole thing was ridiculous. Somehow, in the space of one evening, I'd managed to acquire an incredibly complicated and nonexistent love life.

CHAPTER TEN

I MIXED in a cup of mayonnaise before I realized I was supposed to be making spaghetti salad. I dumped the contents of the bowl into the trash and started over. I had to stop rehearsing lines in my head while working. The character of Edgar was taking over my life— my thoughts, my dreams. After that irritating dinner I'd shared with Mother and Jason, even after the fuss Mary Grace had made about my apartment, I'd dreamed about playing the part of Edgar. The one good thing about Edgar taking over my life, I was starting to get some real insight into the character. I suspected Edgar possessed an inner strength the playwright simply hadn't allowed for. Now, what was the best way to make that inner strength come out?

"Hurry it up back there," Geovanni called from up front.

I cranked open a bottle of Italian dressing. Geovanni never addressed me by name. I wondered if he even remembered what it was. I'd worked here only two months, and I knew I hadn't exactly impressed anyone with my skills during that time. But making salads and refilling vegetables and dressing all day wasn't dazzling work to begin with.

Melanie came dashing through the door, ponytail flying as she tied on her apron. "Sorry I'm late," she mumbled. "What do you need?"

"Can you get those spaghetti noodles from the pot?" I threw a handful of cut veggies into the bowl, grabbed the sausage, and glanced at Mel. The last couple of days, Mel had been edgy. "Are you okay?" I asked. "You seem a little flustered."

"I'm late, that's all."

"You're never late," I pointed out. "You're so punctual, it's scary." I was trying to make a joke, but Mel scowled at me.

"I'm just late, okay? It's not a crime. Let it go."

I couldn't pursue it right then. It was the most hectic time at the restaurant, the lunch rush when office workers poured out of the nearby buildings and placed their orders. It wasn't until well after two that Mel and I could take our own lunch. We sat in what was jokingly referred to as the employee lounge—a windowless alcove with barely enough space for the small table crammed inside it.

"You might as well tell me what's going on," I said. "I'll only pry and prod until you do. So save yourself the annoyance."

Mel hadn't yet touched her food—she was still busy trying to massage the postrush kinks out of her shoulders. "I didn't mean to snap at you earlier. It's just that… I think I'm starting to get involved with someone."

"That's fantastic!"

"No. No, it's not." Mel propped her chin on her hands. Usually she appeared calm and in control, but now she simply looked overwhelmed. Her ponytail was a little lopsided, as if even such a no-nonsense hairstyle had proved too much for her to cope with today. "His name is Toby, and he's very attractive, and he's a student too. Who else would I have time to meet but another student? Anyway, this week we got assigned to work on a project together, except that we kept getting sidetracked talking about all these other things and one thing led to another and… well, last night I actually kissed him when we should have been studying. I don't want to get involved with anyone. Relationships are messy, they take time. Time I don't have. I have goals, Ben. I have things I have to do that don't include worrying about someone's feelings."

"Why do you sound so miserable? Is it really so horrible to take a break from your studies once in a while and enjoy someone's company?"

"No, it's just that… I think about him all the time. He's cluttering my head with crazy notions, and it's affecting my studies."

"Love at first sight, huh?"

"You know damn good and well that's a bullshit fairy tale," Mel grumbled. "I don't even believe in true love, so I have no idea why I'm letting this guy mess my head up so badly."

"Ah, it sounds like the unflappable Mel actually has a romantic bone in her body," I teased.

Mel glared at me. "You're not even the littlest bit funny."

"And that tough exterior of yours is hiding a squishy softness."

"I'm not talking to you anymore."

"Are you writing his name all over your notebook among scribbled hearts and flowers?"

Mel covered her ears and closed her eyes. "La la la. I can't hear you."

I couldn't help but laugh at her childish behavior. I'd have told her just how cute she looked, but she was ignoring me and it was time to get back to work. I let it go, but I'd definitely be bugging her about it later.

We were almost through the rush when Mel came hurrying back to the prep area. She seemed a bit more cheerful. "There's someone out front asking for you."

"Someone... someone for me?"

"Yes, and he's gorgeous. And I do mean gorgeous. Let's see.... Chocolate-brown eyes. Chocolate-brown hair too, except for some fantastic streaks of gray at the temples. Makes him look like he's known trouble and survived. I like that in a man. And what a body...."

I gazed at Mel in dismay. "I don't believe this. You've just described my ex."

Mel raised her eyebrows. "Dude, if that guy really is your ex, I don't know how you ever let him go."

I was tempted to duck out the back door. I didn't want to see Hugh. What was he doing here, anyway? I'd never told him where I worked!

At last, I peered out the small round windows toward the dining room. I couldn't see him.

"It won't hurt to talk to him," Mel said. "He seems very charming and did I mention gorgeous?"

Hugh was extremely handsome and he most certainly could be charming, but I didn't consider that a plus at the moment. I untied my apron, hung it on a hook, and walked out into the restaurant. My momentary urge to hide had vanished. I had never let Hugh intimidate me, and I wasn't about to start now.

He was sitting at a small table by the window. I stood still a moment and just gazed at him, appreciating the dominant lines of his features, the way his hair waved back just so from his stubborn forehead, and yes, the rich chocolate depths of his eyes.

Hugh turned his head, our gazes locked, and I couldn't very well stand there ogling him any longer. I went over to his table.

"Hello, Hugh," I said coolly. "Let me guess. Uncle Johnathan managed to find out where I work and obligingly told you about it."

Hugh gave a shrug that almost seemed good-natured. "I'm the detective this time. I went by your apartment building and spoke to your landlady. She was very helpful, for the right price."

"I'll have to talk to her about that. Maybe she can be just a little less helpful in the future." I was suddenly more pissed at my landlord than I was Hugh. What if she had given that information to some deranged killer? Okay, that was a little dramatic, but the threat of a lawsuit might put a damper on her desire to do it again in the future.

Hugh nodded sagely. "A good idea. You can't have her giving out information to just anyone for a hundred dollars."

"Thank you, I'll be sure to take care of that," I assured him. "If that's all, I really have to get back to work."

"No, you don't. Your friend Melanie said you had a fifteen-minute break coming up."

Hugh was in good form today—taking charge of everyone and everything as usual. I pulled out the chair across from him and sat down. "I'll give you five minutes, that's all. I thought we agreed we weren't going to see each other again?"

"You came to that agreement on your own, right after—"

I held up my hands to silence him. "No need to get into that. What do you want?"

"The first thing I want is to finish this sandwich. It's good. Much better than the kind I make for myself."

I drummed my fingers on the tabletop. "So… how's my mother?"

Hugh had the grace to look a little abashed. "I wouldn't know."

"I'm sure you've spoken with her in the last twenty-four hours. It's just too much of a coincidence otherwise. My mother shows up last night, butting into my life. Now you're doing the same thing. Are you actually going to tell me there's no connection?"

He ate a forkful of potato salad. "I'll admit your mother woke me out of a sound sleep last night. But that's not why I'm here."

I glanced at my watch. "You have four minutes left."

"Go out to dinner with me tonight, Benny."

The way he said my name sent a rush through me. It always had, and I wished he wouldn't call me Benny anymore. "I can't."

"Previous commitment?" Hugh asked in a suspiciously casual voice.

"Mother, of course, told you about what she supposes to be my love life."

He set down the sandwich. "She did mention some guy named Jason. As well as someone else she referred to as 'the mystery man.' Sounds like you have a full social calendar." He gazed at me intently, as if trying to see in me, searching for my secrets. I didn't give up any.

I started to point out that Jason was just a friend but stopped myself. I didn't need to explain myself to Hugh. Glancing at my watch again, I pushed back my chair and stood. "Your five minutes are up," I announced. "It's too bad you wasted a trip all the way from Charleston."

"Dinner, that's all, Ben. I'll wait until you're off work."

I curled my fingers around the back of the chair, remembering what had happened the last time I'd accepted a dinner invitation from him. "I have a rehearsal right after work."

Hugh nodded. "Right. Your uncle told me you'd landed a part. Of course, you could have told me yourself. You have my phone number."

"I didn't think you'd be that interested."

"I'm interested." He continued to hold my gaze.

It took me a second or two to realize I was gripping the back of the chair a bit too hard. I forced my fingers to relax one by one. "So... I have a rehearsal."

"I'm glad you got a part. I know how much it means to you, this acting thing."

Somehow, I always ended up feeling defensive with Hugh. The way he called it my "acting thing"—there was just something dismissive in his tone.

"No, Hugh. I don't think you do know how much it means to me."

"Tell me about it, then. You're the one who's always saying we should talk more." Now he sounded reasonable.

"I used to say that when we were together," I reminded him. "Your timing's a little off. Besides, I don't think you came all this way to chitchat about my acting."

"I came so I could invite you to dinner. That's it. You'll have to eat after your rehearsal, won't you?"

"Sorry, I just can't make it. But tell Mother I said hello." I turned and walked toward the kitchen, making a supreme effort not to spare Hugh another glance. He didn't try to call me back or follow me.

I wondered if it was really going to be this easy to get rid of him.

CHAPTER ELEVEN

WHETHER IT was out of spite or that Jason was simply wearing me down, I'm not sure, but after rehearsal I finally agreed to join him. Not for dinner as he so often requested but for ice cream. I frickin' love ice cream.

"Joyce isn't going to be happy with your changing the layout of the set," I told him as soon as we stepped out of the theater.

"It's going to make things better. Joyce will just have to accept that."

I slid on my sunglasses to shield my eyes from the late-afternoon sun. It was the perfect summer day, midseventies with a slight breeze. "I can't wait to see how that argument turns out. Honestly, Joyce scares me a little."

Jason bumped his shoulder against me. "It's okay, I'll protect you from the mean ol' director."

"I'm not sure you'd win in a head to head," I teased.

"Gee, thanks for the vote of confidence."

"You're welcome." I shoved my hands into my pockets.

"You seemed a little distant during rehearsal. Anything you want to talk about?"

Jason Collins was the last person I could talk to about what had me on edge. I couldn't very well inform him that my ex, a.k.a. the mystery man, had shown up at my job today. I couldn't admit that I'd almost been disappointed when I left work and Hugh wasn't outside waiting for me. No. I couldn't possibly explain the mixture of anticipation and annoyance Hugh inspired in me. Hell, I didn't understand it myself, so how could I expect Jason to?

Instead of answering, I pointed to the sign up ahead. "Is that the place?"

"Yup, the Blue Moon. Best ice cream in the city."

I ordered a double scoop of chocolate chip cookie dough in a waffle cone, and Jason ordered plain vanilla in a cup. I briefly wondered if the boring choice said something about his personality but forgot all about it the instant I got a taste of mine.

"Man, this is delicious."

"Told you." Jason winked. "Hey, there's a table."

Two young girls were just getting up, and Jason and I quickly snagged the spot.

"We need to play the lottery. I come here all the time and I've never gotten a seat."

"Mmm hmm," I agreed, thoroughly enjoying my treat.

"You still haven't told me what's bugging you, but I bet I could guess."

I doubt that. But I didn't meet Jason's gaze. I didn't want to be having this conversation. I just wanted to enjoy the gorgeous summer day and ice cream, and not have to think or talk about anything unpleasant.

Not deterred, Jason continued. "Let's see…. I know that you were married, that your family's rich, that your mom travels around in a limo, and that you don't get along with her very well. It really bothers you that I have so much information on you, doesn't it?"

"I'm just trying to work out a few things in my life. I'm not secretive by nature."

"Then tell me about my competition. Give me a fair chance."

"I'm tired, that's all. It was a busy day at work."

"Okay, you won't talk about yourself, so we'll talk about me," Jason said obligingly. "Did I tell you that last year I almost got engaged?"

"No, you haven't mentioned that yet."

"Well, it's true. I was ready to buy the ring, but Morgan decided he wanted to go to Europe instead. Alone. Depressed the hell out of me—for a while, anyway."

Every now and then, Jason would throw out some detail of his life for discussion. I already knew that his parents had split up when he was ten, that he'd had a lot of girlfriends in junior high but none in high school when he finally came to terms with being gay. I also knew he had three sisters and had majored in theater in college. He was an accessible person. I felt myself relaxing for the first time since Hugh had shown up at the restaurant.

"I'm sorry about your engagement," I said with true sincerity. "But you really do seem to have recovered."

"So maybe he wasn't the right man for me. Morgan, that is. But he's all in the past. After him came George."

"Wait a minute. I thought your last boyfriend was someone named Dennis."

"Right. But George was post-Morgan and pre-Dennis."

"Did you throw George over, or was it the other way around?"

"Ben, I've told you I never throw a man over. Too risky a proposition. I just hang around until they get tired of me. I like seeing you like this, by the way."

"How do you mean?"

"Smiling. Enjoying yourself. I've watched you this past week, and it's occurred to me that you don't enjoy yourself a lot."

I frowned at him. "What a strange thing to say. Of course I enjoy myself. That's the whole point of my new life."

Jason took another bite of ice cream while he studied me. "Just the way you say that, 'the whole point of your life.' It's like you're frantic, racing around even though you haven't figured out yet where you're going."

I had much preferred it when we'd been talking about Jason. "I beg to differ. These days I know exactly where I'm going."

"And where's that?"

With one simple question, Jason had me asking myself whether I really did know. I knew I wanted to act and that I had to grab my chance while I could. Beyond that, I wasn't sure.

I didn't have an answer to his question, so instead I held up my cone. "I'm going to the gym after I eat every last bite of this."

Jason raked his eyes over me, then smiled. "Now, that I'd like to see."

"Well, watch." I took a big bite and munched happily on a chunk of cookie dough.

"That's not what I meant. I was talking about you in the gym, all sweaty, muscles bulging."

I couldn't help but laugh. I was a runt. There was nothing bulging on me except when I popped a boner. "Bulging muscles? You really are a charmer."

"Happiness looks good on you. My new mission in life is to make you laugh as often as possible."

We finished our ice cream, making small talk and laughing. For a little while, not a single negative thought popped into my head. It was fun and I was truly enjoying myself. Jason really was quite charming.

But of course, Jason couldn't help himself from prodding me on the walk back to the theater. "So, what's the deal with this mystery man?

"I should have known," I muttered. "You're just had to ruin my happy vibe, didn't you?"

"Mystery man doesn't make you happy?"

"I didn't say that…." My voice trailed off. We'd reached the outside of the theater, and I glanced around. Then I glanced around again, more carefully.

"You're looking for him, aren't you?" Jason asked. "The man who never shows up."

"Of course not," I insisted.

"He doesn't make you happy."

"Who?" I asked absently.

"The man who never shows up," Jason clarified. "That's what I was talking about earlier, how you don't seem to enjoy yourself very much. It must be because of him."

"Right, the mystery man," I said in a caustic tone. "Look, Jason—"

"If you're going to tell me your life is complicated, I've already heard that part."

"You won't let a person get away with anything, will you?" I said ruefully.

"Not when I'm interested in a person." He moved closer to me and put his arm around my shoulders. It seemed a casual gesture, and I even felt comfortable with Jason's arm around me. But how comfortable should I get with him? Was it really fair to encourage Jason's advances when my head was so screwed up and my heart…? Well, my heart was just as messed up.

"Ben." It was Hugh's voice. Low, deep, resonating along my nerve endings. I twisted around, slipping away from Jason's half embrace.

I started to curse him out but snapped my mouth shut at the last second. Hugh constantly sneaking up on me was getting old really fast. It didn't matter that I was excited to see him and that part of me was jumping for joy. It was just proof of how mental I'd become. For a few seconds, I glared at him, even though his face remained in shadow. It wasn't really necessary to see him. I felt his presence. Hugh strolled confidently toward me, his eyes boring into me. He dominated my senses, my emotions. When the silence threatened to grow awkward, I did my best to get myself back under control. No small feat, but I was supremely proud of myself when my voice came out clear and strong as I said, "Jason, this is Hugh Bayard. Hugh, Jason Collins."

They shook hands only briefly, not saying a word, seeming to size each other up. I was left to fill another silence. I felt obligated to fill it. "So, Hugh, I didn't expect to see you here." It wasn't an outright lie. I had hoped, but expected? No.

"My dinner offer is still open."

"I doubt he's hungry—we just came back from ice cream," Jason put in.

I glared at Jason. "I can speak for myself, thank you very much." I hated when people did that. Jason had the good sense to look properly chastised. Of course, that only made Hugh smile smugly. I swallowed down my sigh. What I should have done was turn Hugh down. Then I could have gone home, locked myself in my apartment, and studied my lines. I could have kept company with Edgar, the recluse uncle.

"Hugh and I have a few things to discuss," I said before thinking better of it. It wasn't what I'd meant to say. I meant to turn Hugh down, but obviously my brain hadn't gotten the memo.

"Well, good night, then. I'll see you tomorrow," Jason said, not sounding the least bit happy.

"Sure. Tomorrow," I agreed.

Jason and Hugh nodded at each other. I followed Hugh across the street to his car. With him, I always felt as if I were being pulled along by his dominant presence. One step behind like the good little submissive I should be.

Screw that!

I caught up quickly and snatched the passenger door open before Hugh could, and I climbed inside. Hugh gave me a strange look, then shrugged and closed the door. I glanced through the side window toward the theater. Jason was still standing there on the sidewalk, watching. I turned away and stared straight ahead.

Hugh got in beside me, fired up the engine, and pulled out onto the road. Hugh didn't speak, and he didn't ask me where I'd like to go for dinner. It occurred to me that if it was Jason, he would have at least asked my opinion on what type of food I wanted, and there certainly wouldn't be this uncomfortable silence. By now Jason would have been making some joke about having won my favor for the evening before going a mile a minute about his life or probing cheerfully into mine. Funny, I could surmise all these things about Jason Collins after having known him only a short while, yet never knew what Hugh was thinking or doing after knowing him all these years.

"Hugh, do you ever wonder what I'm thinking?"

Hugh glanced at me, then concentrated on his driving. "That's a peculiar question."

"Not really. Take tonight, for instance. You showed up at the theater, even though I told you I didn't want to see you again. Did you do it just because of what you wanted, or were you actually speculating that I wanted you to show up?"

Hugh seemed to give this some consideration. "This may surprise you, Ben, but I've often wondered during the past year if you're happy, if you're finding what you want. But as far as tonight, I wanted to see you, and I figured the worst thing that could happen was

79

you'd say no. You're looking for confirmation that I'm insensitive, arrogant…. What else did you use to call me?"

"Dictatorial," I supplied. "And feudal—I think I called you that once too."

"Ah yes, now I remember. Does the opinion still stand?"

Now I was the one who needed a minute to think things over. "Yes," I said finally. "I'm afraid it does."

When I looked at Hugh, there was a ghost of a smile curling his upper lip. At least I thought I saw one. It was difficult to tell in the dim interior of the car.

As Hugh maneuvered deftly through traffic, I compared him to Jason once again. Being with Jason was nice, the conversation easy. With Hugh, tension dominated. I was always trying to guess what he was thinking, and the conversation was forced. When had that happened? I remembered a time when Hugh and I talked with that same ease. Hadn't we? We must have—or was I blinded by my love for Hugh? I wasn't sure anymore. All I knew was that now, everything with Hugh was strict, refined, strangling. "Let me guess where you're taking me. It will be a restaurant we've never been to together, but it will be very elegant. Of course, you won't even notice how impossibly elegant it is because you're so accustomed to that type of thing."

"You keep trying to pretend that your background is different from mine. There's a certain snobbery in that, even if you are living in a dive."

"Don't you have something disparaging to say about the theater?"

"Okay, that's a dive too," Hugh said gruffly. "But I'm still glad you got your break. And I'd like to see your play."

That was a disturbing notion—Hugh watching me perform. Just the thought of him being in the audience someday made me uncomfortable. I didn't know what to say to that, so I simply stared out the window without seeing anything. I was suddenly on edge and regretting my decision of allowing Hugh to take me to dinner. The midtown traffic jam only added to my ill mood. By the time we arrived at the restaurant, the stress had knotted my muscles. I tried rolling my neck, but it only popped and cracked without doing anything to relieve the tension.

No surprise, the Italian restaurant Hugh had chosen was elegant. I refrained from rolling my eyes as the maître d' showed us to our table but just barely. This was so typical Hugh. I'd always believed it was such a waste of money when the same meal, and a damn good one, could be obtained for a quarter of the price.

"You're a long way from Charleston. Are you going to tell me why you came all this way?"

"I already told you. I wanted to go to dinner with you. And here we are."

"You're so full of it."

"You don't believe me, Benny?" His voice always went a little husky when he called me that. Could he possibly know the effect it had on me? For my sake, I hoped not.

"No, I don't. You've been taking an awful lot of time away from the office these days. It's not like you."

"I've been giving more duties to Martin lately. He's become quite capable." Martin Schuler was his assistant. He'd been with Hugh for ten years. He'd been more than capable about six months after he started. "Besides," Hugh continued, "I had anticipated being off for your mother's wedding, so there isn't much I'm missing."

I should have known Hugh wasn't taking time away from his precious office for me. He never did. I hid my disappointment behind my menu. I wasn't hungry, but knowing Hugh as I did, he'd just try to order for me, anyway. When the server arrived at the table, I quickly ordered the chicken alfredo—it could be easily warmed up later—and a Coke. No way was I taking a sip of alcohol. I'd already proven it was a bad idea to drink when I was around Hugh. I had learned from my mistake. It didn't matter that the last time we hooked up I was stone-cold sober. I still had a hard time resisting Hugh, but I was working on it.

As soon as the waiter moved away, Hugh said, "From the look of things, you seem to be getting along pretty well with that Collins fellow."

"It's easy to get along with Jason. Not that it's really any of your—"

"But I'd like to know something about this mystery man I've heard of."

I stifled a curse. The mystery man was starting to have a life all his own. "You should know by now to ignore anything my mother says. She always exaggerates."

Hugh studied me across the table. His eyes seemed even darker than usual. "Something tells me that Collins isn't the real danger. It's this other man, the one you won't talk about."

"Danger? That's an interesting way to put it."

"He's the one you care about, isn't he?" Hugh persisted. "You might as well tell me, Ben. You never could keep a secret."

I made a sound that was somewhere between a groan and a laugh, and which did not at all adequately express my frustration. "Just leave it alone. I'm not going to talk about it to you or Jason or—"

"So, Collins is worried about this mystery man too? Hmm, all the more proof."

I wanted to yell, but somehow I kept my voice at a moderate level. "Proof of what? Why are you suddenly so curious about my love life, Hugh? It's been a year. Don't you think it's time to move on?"

"Tell me about the mystery man," Hugh said, completely ignoring my questions.

I picked up my water glass and took a sip to wet my suddenly dry throat. Hugh was so damn curious about the mystery man. Fine. He was going to get an earful, and I'd be damned if I'd sugarcoat it. "You asked for it."

CHAPTER TWELVE

JUST THEN, the server arrived at our table with a tray heavily laden with pasta, salad, and bread, and I had a few more minutes to decide what I was going to say. The scent of savory garlic and parmesan cheese wafted up from the plate of chicken alfredo. It smelled too good not to at least try it. I twirled my fork in the pasta and took a small bite. The thick cream sauce was delicious.

"So this mystery man," Hugh prompted before popping a large bite of steak into his mouth.

"Well, to be honest he is a very difficult person." I took a swig of Coke before I continued. "He's not the most talkative person nor does he like to share his feelings. I sometimes wonder if he even has any. Other times… well, other times I know that of course he has to have them. But how deeply he feels about things, I don't know because he is pretty closed off. I wish I knew why."

"This mystery man… sounds familiar."

"Does he?" I frowned a little. "I'd really like to get to know him, but it's like he hides who he really is behind a mask. I'm always trying to guess how he feels."

"A real forthcoming person, your mystery man." Hugh moved his food around his plate with his fork. "Sounds like he's earned his name. But maybe you should give him a little more credit. Maybe he shows his concern, instead of talking about it all the time."

"You're taking his side?" Talking about the mystery man enabled me to step away a little from my own life, as if I were standing back to watch us interacting. What did I see? Two people who could never seem to come to agreement on what love meant. Two people with different needs. I wanted openness and unapologetic devotion. Hugh wanted a partner who wouldn't constantly probe his emotions. Yes. We were two very different people.

"I do believe he's concerned about me, this mystery man. I believe he cares about me in a certain way. But it's just not enough. I want more than his concern. I want… passion. Not just the physical kind, though. I'm talking about emotional passion. I just don't know if he has that to give me, or anyone. Maybe it's just not in his nature."

Hugh studied me very carefully. Did he understand what I was trying to say? With Hugh, it was impossible to know. True to form, he kept his deepest reactions from me. "So what are you going to do, Ben? Will you try to turn this man into your ideal partner?"

"No. True change has to come from within. He first has to recognize the need to do so, then desire to do so."

Hugh suddenly seemed more interested in his meal than the conversation. He'd always done that in the past, ignored me when any topic bothered him. Which usually meant it had to do with those pesky emotions. It was so damn frustrating, and honestly, I had no idea why I continued to put myself through the misery. Hugh wasn't going to change. He was what he was, and I either had to learn to accept it, give in to the physical desires my body craved and ignore my heart and mind, or walk away once and for all.

The silence was heavy. The meal was now like sludge on my tongue, and I had a difficult time swallowing it down. Hugh had no such problem and cleaned his plate as well as the bread and salad.

"If you're still hungry, you're welcome to mine."

Hugh stared at my plate for a second. I could tell he wanted it, but he shook his head. "Thanks, but I know how much you like your leftovers. You're the only person I know who thinks pasta tastes better the next day."

"It does. The pasta soaking in the sauce all night. Delish! I'm sure I'm not the only one who thinks so, but I am surprised you even noticed."

"I notice a lot more than you think," Hugh said.

"Really?" I wasn't sure if that was true, at least not when it came to me. Then again, if Hugh knew such a trivial thing about me, how could he not know the important things? It was a question I wasn't

84

going to find the answers to anytime soon. I'd been contemplating it for years.

I had my dinner boxed up, and we left the restaurant. Hugh drove me to my apartment. The silence went with us.

When Hugh pulled up to my building, I glanced at him. "Thanks for the great conversation and dinner," I said snappishly.

"I'm walking you up to your apartment."

"Sorry, bud, not this time."

"Ben, this is a lousy neighborhood. I'm going to walk you to your door and make sure you get in okay. That's all."

If I remembered correctly, those were almost the exact words Hugh had used the first time—the night he'd come to tell me about my mother's wedding. The next morning I'd woken up with Hugh in my bed, all because I had allowed him to walk me to my door.

"Forget it." I opened the door and stepped out of the car. My decision wasn't open for discussion, just as Hugh's emotions hadn't been. I needed to be away from him, needed time to process. I hurried into my building and up the first flight of rickety stairs. The elevator was out again, but I didn't trust it much even on its good days. The building had at least one pretense of safety—bare bulbs hung from a cord on each landing. Unfortunately, the wiring looked frayed and the lights often flickered.

I hadn't even made it to the first landing when Hugh reached my side.

"Dammit, Hugh! Why do you have to be such a pain in my ass?"

"Just part of my charm." Hugh winked.

I stood and glared at him for a second. I debated about whether to stand my ground and refuse to budge until Hugh left. From the determined glint in his eye, he wasn't going anywhere anytime soon. Bastard. I could be stubborn too. Hugh could follow me all he wanted, but I'd be damned if I'd let him into my apartment.

I tromped up the stairs, passing the second floor... the third...

"Ben, would it be so bad if you took some money from your trust fund for a decent place to live? Would that really destroy your independence?"

"This is good exercise."

Fourth story… fifth… sixth…

"Everyone is born with certain advantages and disadvantages," Hugh argued. "It makes sense to use what you're given."

"It makes sense to find out what you can do on your own."

Seventh… eighth… ninth….

We were both breathing heavily by the time we reached the tenth floor. I was pleased to see that I seemed to be in just as good of shape as Hugh. I worked the locks on my door. Before I opened it, I turned around to face Hugh.

"Okay, I'm safe. Thank you for walking me to my door."

"Ben…." Hugh ran the back of his knuckles along my jaw. "I worry about you living here."

With that simple gesture, a tingling sensation raced down my spine. I pressed into Hugh's touch. "I'll make sure my doors are locked. You probably should go." Protest was coming out of my mouth, but my hands were reaching to pull Hugh into an embrace.

Hugh leaned down and pressed his lips to mine. I opened to him, welcoming him in, giving as good as I was getting. I tightened my hold on him as I explored his mouth with my tongue. As the kiss deepened, I pressed harder against Hugh's muscular body. He pressed me against the rough wood of the door. Kissing him was as easy as breathing, and I couldn't get enough. My brain short-circuited, and pure carnal lust rushed through me at a dizzying speed. Every cell in my body craved him. I was addicted to him. Being an addict was rarely a good thing. The realization brought back some of my common sense.

I dragged my mouth away and pressed my forehead against his chest. My breath came in short pants, and it took me a second to solidify my new resolve. I would not be Hugh's junkie. "You need to go," I finally said.

"I want you." Hugh ground his erection against mine. "You want me. Don't deny us what we need."

I lifted my head and stared at him. "So you showed up and walked me to my door just so you could fuck me again?"

Hugh scowled, but it didn't hide the lust that was still shining in his dark eyes. "You know there is a lot more to us than fucking, as you so crudely put it. And what's so horrible about wanting to share your bed? We're very good at it."

"You haven't changed, Hugh. You never will and quite honestly, neither will I." With the only shred of willpower I had left, I turned and slipped inside my apartment. I closed the door on a startled Hugh and engaged the locks. I leaned my forehead against the doorjamb and closed my eyes. I knew he still waited on the other side. I was thrumming, my cock achingly hard. My traitorous body fought against my will, but somehow, I stayed where I was. I didn't reach for the lock. I didn't open the door. After what felt like an eternity, I finally heard the sound of footsteps receding down the hall… away from me.

I turned, pressed my back against the door, and slid down till I was sitting. My pulse had finally slowed as had my breathing, but I was shaken. I'd nearly given in to Hugh again. I hated how weak I was around him. I hated that I didn't know how to stop even more.

JASON TOSSED a large straw hat toward me as if it were a Frisbee. "Try that. Looks like something Edgar would wear."

I put the hat on my head, then picked up a 1950s-style hand mirror to study the effect. "No way! Edgar would see this hat as silly. That's the last thing he wants to be. He's very concerned about how others see him."

"Hmm, nonsilly, huh? Okay, let me try again." Jason muttered as he disappeared down one of the crowded aisles of the thrift shop.

Since it was my day off, Jason had suggested a shopping expedition, while really all I wanted to do was hide away in my apartment, put my feet up, and take a break from the craziness my life had become. But I hadn't been able to say no when he insisted the outing was necessary in order to outfit my character.

Now I was glad I came. I was having a great time. I loved this place. It was filled with vintage clothing, secondhand furniture, toys from modern to antique, dishes, knickknacks, and a huge collection of old 45s and LPs.

Jason reappeared with a top hat. "Less silly?"

"Definitely less silly, but Edgar wouldn't wear it. He's reserved not pompous. He knows he would look ridiculous wearing that thing. He'd want something refined yet subtle."

"C'mon, show me what you mean." Jason grabbed my hand and pulled me along with him as he went off on another exploration. Oddly, it was comforting holding hands with him.

"Here you go," Jason announced and gestured toward the rack. "Pick one of these. Then I'll have a better idea of what type of hat you, I mean, Edgar will need."

I released Jason's hand and lifted one from the rack and surveyed it—a 1930s style. "Yes," I murmured. I ran my fingers gently over the brim. Edgar would wear something exactly like this.

"I knew we'd find something here." Jason smiled. "Now I know exactly what you need—a fedora." He took my hand, and this time I allowed him to entwine his fingers in mine.

"Yes! Exactly what Edgar would wear."

We walked hand in hand through the clothing section. Jason pulled a black fedora from a mannequin and placed it on my head. It fit perfectly. I adjusted the hat, giving it a bit of a gangster tilt. Jason nodded appreciatively. I rolled my eyes and set the hat correctly, then laughed.

We moved on to the furniture section. I spotted a high-backed sofa with frayed cushions. I glanced at the price tag. "Reasonable. Not that Edgar would ever own a piece of furniture like this. He prides himself on having more sophisticated tastes."

"I've created a monster. All you've talked about today is Edgar." His tone was light and teasing.

"I thought that was the whole idea. We're here to get more familiar with our characters' personalities. But you haven't found anything for Pete yet."

"Pete is more Upper East Side. He wouldn't be caught dead in a place like this. Besides, I didn't bring you here just so you could wallow in Edgar. I thought it was a clever way to make you spend more time with me." Jason gave me an engaging smile. "I figured I'd work my way up to being allowed to take you to dinner."

Yes was on the tip of my tongue. I really did enjoy spending time with Jason. He made me laugh. Sure, he could be a bit persistent, but never in a threatening way. I was flattered by Jason's attentions. He was handsome, shared my passion for the theater, and had no issues about sharing his feelings with me. I liked that. I never had to guess. Jason wore his heart on his sleeve. He was all the things I wanted in a man. So why was I hesitating in accepting Jason's dinner invitation?

"I wonder which one you're thinking about, the ex or the mystery man?" Jason asked, pulling me from my musings.

"What makes you think that?"

"You get this faraway look at times." Jason shrugged. "I figure you were probably thinking about one of them."

"I don't always think about men, ya know. Sometimes, I get lost in thought about cats."

"What! Cats? Seriously?"

"Sure, why not? I love cats." I chuckled and slipped my hand from Jason's and strolled away.

Of course I hadn't been thinking about felines, but it was the first thing that had popped into my head. I couldn't admit that I'd been thinking about him. It would do no good. Jason was a great guy. I couldn't lead him on. I couldn't give him what he was looking for when I was still so conflicted about my feelings for Hugh. I flat out refused to be in a relationship in which I couldn't give the other person what they needed. I knew firsthand how painful that could be.

Jason caught up, walking at my side as we made our way through the shop. "I like cats too," he admitted. "I think they are a great first pet, low maintenance. A couple can learn a lot about each other from the way they care for them."

"You should get one," I suggested.

"We should," Jason countered.

"Umm, no. Friends can share a lot of things, but ownership of a pet isn't one of them."

"Friends?"

"Sure, it's a good place to start. I'm not rushing into anything."

"That's a hint to back off if I've ever heard one. But taking things slow is always a mistake."

"It's the other way around," I objected. "From the sound of it, you always rush into relationships too quickly. I mean, there was George and Dennis and…. Who's the other one?"

"Morgan. He's the one who left me for Europe," Jason explained.

"Anyway, if you hadn't rushed it, maybe you would have figured out Morgan wasn't right for you and you'd have saved yourself a lot of trouble."

"If we did it your way, Ben, people would be so sensible they'd never fall in love. They'd save themselves a lot of pain, but a lot of happiness too."

"That's not such a bad idea," I muttered. I was all for trading a little happiness if it meant the pain and heartbreak would cease.

"Are you really such a cynic? Which one made you that way, the ex or the mystery man?" Jason asked.

I suspected Jason would be happy to have a prolonged discussion about it. He seemed to relish in-depth discussions. "Let's go buy some more things for Edgar."

Jason grabbed my hand. He held my gaze, the expression on his face one of curiosity. I was obviously the puzzle he was trying to solve. "I wonder what it would take to get him out of your head," he murmured, leaning in slightly. "Whichever one it is…."

Jason leaned in more and pressed his lips to mine. I don't know if it was shock that he was kissing me in public—Hugh would never do such a thing—or if part of me wanted Jason to kiss me. Whichever it was, I allowed it. It was a very pleasant kiss. It didn't overpower or overwhelm. It just felt good, and that was precisely why I stepped back so quickly.

Jason's smile was rueful. "Obviously it'll take more than that to make you forget him."

"Jason—"

"I wish I could make you forget." For a moment, Jason looked almost somber.

I wished he could too.

CHAPTER THIRTEEN

THE DOOR swung open and Geovanni stepped into the kitchen and headed straight for me. From the disapproving expression on my boss's face, whatever he wanted couldn't be good. I tensed, wondering what I'd done wrong.

"There is a messenger out front insisting he deliver a package to you and no one else."

"Me?"

"Is that not what I said?"

"Yes, sir." I wiped my hands on my apron and hurried out into the dining room. A courier was standing at the register, chatting with Mel. I approached them. "Hi, I understand you have something for me? I'm Benson Winthrop."

The courier handed me an envelope, winked at Mel, and vanished out the door.

Intrigued, I gazed down at the envelope. It bore no handwriting, no clue to its sender. I broke open the seal and found no letter inside. There was only a single theater ticket.

Mel glanced over my shoulder. "Oh. My. God. I'd love to see that show, except that I'd have to stop eating for a week to afford it."

"You're exaggerating." I turned the ticket over in my fingers. Broadway! Holy shit, Mel wasn't exaggerating.

"Any idea who sent it?" Mel asked. Impossibly nosy, she took the ticket from me and examined it. "Pretty convenient, I'd say. It's for tomorrow night. You don't have a rehearsal then. It's almost like someone knew your schedule."

I still didn't speak, lost in my own thoughts. That ticket, arriving in a plain, tasteful envelope, had aroused an unsettling mixture of doubt and suspense in me.

Mel, meanwhile, went on without any encouragement. "Very interesting. You know, this ticket is almost like… a lure. Someone's just cast a line, and I'm fairly certain you're the fish."

"Don't be ridiculous," I said, snatching the ticket back from her. "You have an overactive imagination."

"I don't think so. I suspect I'm right on." Mel looked at me expectantly. "The only question is… will you take the bait?"

THE FOLLOWING evening, I sat in my apartment, holding the theater ticket and debating whether or not to tear it into pieces. If I was smart, that was exactly what I'd do. I'd tear it into pieces, and then I'd spend a quiet evening at home studying my lines.

But it was Broadway. How could I not go?

How could I go?

There was part of me that had a sneaking suspicion Jason had sent it. *It's almost like someone knew your schedule.* He was the only one besides Mel who knew it. Then there was another part of me, a larger part, hoping it had been Hugh. But if it was, then surely he was playing a game. If I went to the theater, well, it would be as if Hugh had snapped his fingers and I obeyed.

Torn, I tossed the ticket down on the coffee table. I wasn't even sure which one I wanted it to be.

That was not true. I wanted it to be Hugh who had sent it— for the reasons that Jason would have sent it—because he wanted to make me happy and hear me laugh.

I stood up and paced around the small space, debating all the pros and cons of going to the theater. Then I turned and went into the bedroom and rummaged through my closet. I wasn't going to try to figure it out one way or the other—Jason, Hugh—all I knew was I was going to the theater.

The contents of my closet were sparse, but I pulled out the suit I'd intended to wear to Mother's wedding. It would have to do because it was all I had. When I'd left Hugh, I'd also left behind all the things acquired through Hugh or the Winthrop dollar. So basically, everything I owned.

Irritation was the flavor of the day, but it was now mixed with a healthy dose of nervous energy that made me jittery. I stepped into the shower and stood beneath the warm flow of water for long moments but couldn't seem to quell my excitement. I was literally vibrating with anticipation. Soon, I'd see Hugh again. I froze. Damn Hugh Bayard! Why in the hell couldn't I let him go? I stayed in the shower until the water turned cold. If I'd been hoping that by delaying I would come to my senses, I was sorely disappointed.

I turned off the taps and quickly dried off. I swiped my hand over the fogged mirror, shaved, and did my best to control my mop of hair—a nearly impossible feat. I really did need a haircut, but I managed. Finally, I slid into my suit jacket and was on my way out the bedroom door when I hesitated, returned to the bureau, and picked up my one small bottle of cologne. I dabbed some on, then wondered if it was too much. If the theater was overly warm or my nerves got the better of me, I'd be sweating and stinking—not a good combination. But it was too late to worry about that. I hurried out to the other room, grabbed the ticket, and went down to hail a cab.

I arrived in the theater district near Times Square. All the old excitement kicked in for me when I saw the marquees blazing with lights, the dusky sky a backdrop—just like the first time I'd been here, the childlike wonder. The dazzling lights still made me think of the magic roused in me by brightly spinning carousels.

Of course, during the past months, I had not attended a single Broadway show. On my meager salary, I simply couldn't afford such an indulgence.

The cab deposited me in front of the Barrett Theater. I entered the crowded lobby and found myself surrounded by a streamlined luxury, and the contrast to the scruffy Stewart Mott Playhouse could not have been starker. Out of nowhere, my stomach flipped, nausea threatened. I shouldn't have come. I didn't want to see either of them, not when I was so screwed up. I should go. I need to go. I turned.

Then I saw him.

Not Hugh… but Jason, looking handsome in jacket and tie, standing across the lobby, a little separate from the other patrons, with a mischievous smile on his face. Jason had sent the ticket?

My first reaction—piercing disappointment. My second, excitement. My third, an attempt to cover up my initial one as Jason walked toward me. By the time he reached me, I managed a smile.

"Very clever. You really are a good actor. The whole 'poor me, it would cost me a week's salary' was quite convincing," I said.

Jason returned the smile. Yet he looked skeptical. "I was hoping you'd pick up on that, but I admit I was worried you'd be disappointed it wasn't him."

"Him who? With all these men in my life, it really could have been anyone, I suppose," I said lightly.

"I am but one of many," he sighed dramatically. I was sure that was for affect as well.

"Yes, but you're the one who won out tonight." I touched his arm, my smile growing. "It's a very nice surprise. Sneaky but very romantic."

I really had been hoping for a romantic gesture from Hugh, not Jason. I'd ignored the fact that my ex was notoriously unromantic.

"So does this send me to the top of this list of your many suitors?"

"For tonight, it does."

Jason laid his hand over his heart. "You wound me, Ben. The fact that I'm now going to have to starve for the next week, I would have thought that would put me there for more than a night."

"Are you trying to make me feel sorry for you?"

"A little. Is it working?"

"Not in the least. But seeing as you sacrificed so much, hopefully it will be worth it."

Jason's gaze traveled over me appreciatively. "It already is. You look especially handsome tonight."

"Stop it, you already got the date." I bumped my shoulder against Jason as we went through the crowd and into the auditorium. "Thank you, for… well, just thank you."

Jason had arranged for excellent seats, close enough to the stage for a perfect view, but not too close that the orchestra would be a distraction. As I settled into my plush seat, I thought once again of the playhouse with its rows of tatty old velvet chairs.

Then the auditorium lights went down, the curtain went up, the orchestra began to play, and I tried to forget everything but the pageantry before me. *Quivira* was the boisterous, appealing tale of a band of explorers in search of a mythical city in eighteenth-century Texas. The music was catchy, the singing superb, the story touching.

Even as I became caught up in the play, I couldn't seem to stop thinking about Hugh. I realized how few times we'd attended the theater when we were together. Hugh spent so many late nights at the office, for one thing. Besides, the theater was my activity, not Hugh's. In what little spare time he had, he preferred physical activities such as hiking, riding, tennis. He wasn't one to sit around and watch others perform. Even though I'd been sure to join him in the things he liked to do, he never returned the favor. I had gone to plays with friends or by myself.

When the curtains came down at intermission, Jason glanced at me. "Enjoying yourself?"

"Oh, of course. This is fantastic. I can't thank you enough."

"You sound like you're reading a speech," Jason said. "You know, whenever I'm with you, I feel like there's three of us. You, me… and the guy who makes you unhappy."

"He's not here with us right now," I said firmly. "We can have a perfectly good time without him. We are having a good time."

"You say that often enough, maybe you'll convince one of us."

I gazed at him in exasperation. "Are you always so observant?"

"Generally. But you're easy to read. Your face is very expressive." With that, Jason escorted me out to the lobby for a glass of wine.

As I sipped my wine, I made an effort to concentrate on Jason. He really did look good. I suspected he'd taken special care with his attire. I had never seen Jason in a jacket before. His sandy hair curled at his collar, and his hazel eyes reminded me of the color of leaves just starting to turn in the fall. He was attentive, standing here with me, embellishing his latest argument with Joyce in an effort to make me laugh. Jason gave the impression that there was nowhere else he would rather be right now than here with me. Hugh had never made me feel like that, as if I possessed all his attention, all his focus. I had always pictured Hugh's mind as being compartmentalized—one small room in it for me and quite a large room for Bayard Investments. There was only one activity during which I had ever felt I had Hugh's complete participation and that was during sex. Christ, even when clicking off Hugh's faults, I couldn't stop from finding some good in him.

I watched the people around me, concentrated on the buttery and oaky flavor of the chardonnay, on Jason, anything to keep my mind from wandering beyond the here and now. It really didn't work, so it was a relief when we headed back into the auditorium. We took our seats, and the orchestra started up again.

During the performance, Jason reached over in the most natural way possible and took my hand. I didn't pull away. I allowed our fingers to remain clasped for several moments. It was pleasant, holding hands with Jason in the darkened theater. It was also a comforting. As soon as I realized just how comforting it was, I slipped my fingers away. I didn't want to be unfair to him. I didn't want to use him for some type of consolation.

As the play went on, I actually managed to lose myself in it, and I regretted the moment when the curtain fell for the last time. It occurred to me that going to the theater had been another type of comfort and consolation for me. Was it any coincidence that during the worst times in my relationship with Hugh, I had attended as many plays and movies as I could?

Jason and I took a cab to my apartment. The elevator was still out, so we had to climb the nine flights of stairs. I remembered that night a week ago when I had climbed these same stairs with Hugh. We'd been breathless by the time we'd reached my apartment.

And now here I was with another man, reaching my doorway, breathless again. Once again I unbolted the locks. And once again a man took me in his arms. I allowed him to hold me, pressed my cheek against Jason's shoulder. This time my breathing quieted down, became steady and even. Not like the other night....

"Thank you for taking me to the theater and walking me to my door. I had a really nice time."

"Uh-oh. when a man tells you that he had a *nice* time, you know you blew it."

I couldn't help smiling. "I'm afraid you have a streak of melodrama in you. What on earth is wrong with having a nice time?"

"It's like saying you had vanilla pudding for dessert instead of cherries jubilee. It's like saying you took a nap instead of going skydiving. It's like saying—"

"Okay, I get the message. But I did have a nice time. A great time, even. Does that satisfy you?"

His arms tightened around me. "I'm not feeling exactly satisfied right now, Ben. You see... I think I'm falling for you."

This, at last, made me draw back. I studied Jason in dismay. "Don't say that. You're always falling for someone too quickly. With George and Dennis and—"

"This feels different," Jason said somberly.

"Please don't say that," I implored. "I enjoy spending time with you. You make me laugh, and Lord knows I need laughter in my life right now. I just... I don't know if I can return those feelings to anyone right now."

"Except him." Jason stated the words flatly, and Hugh almost seemed to materialize between us.

I held Jason's gaze and tried to be as honest as I could. "I don't know what I'm feeling, and until I sort things out, it wouldn't be fair to anyone, including myself, to enter into another relationship." I shook my head. "I can't, not right now."

"I can respect that, but you can't blame a guy for trying."

"Nope, but I hope you'll keep making me laugh. It's a nice way to balance out the stress."

"I'd like nothing better. Well…." I pointed a warning finger. Jason shrugged, a playful smile on his handsome face. He then pressed a gentle kiss to my cheek. "Good night, Ben."

"Good night, see you tomorrow." I went into my apartment, locked the door, and once again heard a man's footsteps retreating down the hall.

CHAPTER FOURTEEN

MEL SEEMED oddly keyed up. She sat across from me in the employee lounge, creasing a paper napkin over and over in her hands. Her expression, normally so calm, was one of suppressed excitement. Instead of her usual ponytail, she wore her hair loose, allowing it to fall past her shoulders. She'd curled it. It was totally out of character for Mel. She never bothered to style her hair. She'd once told me that she'd rather get in an extra thirty minutes of studying than fuss with a blow-dryer and curlers. Obviously, something had changed her mind.

"Cute hairdo," I complimented.

Mel flipped a curl over her shoulder. "I was running late."

"Wow, you mean it takes longer to curl it than it does to put it up in a pony? I wouldn't have known."

"Shut up." Mel threw her napkin at me. "That problem I told you about before, well, it's not really such a problem after all. I got an A on my psych exam."

"And Toby?"

Mel nodded. "Toby and I… things have advanced a little."

"Ooh, you're banging?"

"Would you like to hear about it? I can totally give you a play-by-play," Mel offered, waggling her brows.

I held up my hands as if to ward off an evil being. "No! No! No! Anything that has to do with the va-jay-jay is an off-limits topic whenever I'm around,"

"Fine, then I won't tell you it's"—she held her hands about ten inches apart—"this big."

"Good Lord, no wonder it was lust at first sight." I threw the napkin back at her, but she dodged just in time and it went flying past her.

Mel winked, then took her hairnet from her pocket and grimaced at it. "If I don't wear this, the boss will have a fit. But do you think it will flatten me down too much?"

I stared at her. With her hair falling in those soft curls past her shoulders, she suddenly looked vulnerable. Wow, maybe it was more than just lust. This Toby must be quite the guy if he could pry Mel away from her studies even for a moment. And to have her worried about her hair? Yeah, she had it bad for him.

"I have no idea, but I'm sure you'll be cute curly or flat."

"Great, now I'm going to have to get a new stylist. I wasn't going for cute." Mel stuck her tongue out at me, then hurried back to work.

I remained seated a moment longer. I was a bit envious of Mel. I remembered what first love felt like. You think about them all the time, your belly flutters every time you see them, and when they touch you… damn!

Kind of how you feel about Hugh. Yeah, well, hopefully this Toby guy felt the same about Mel. And hopefully he told her how he felt, because if he didn't… yeah, Mel was screwed.

Well, at least I could provide understanding and a shoulder to cry on if he turned out to be like Hugh. While misery loves company, I wouldn't wish that on her. Not even for the chance to have a comrade in understanding. I really hoped, for Mel's sake, Toby was more like Jason when it came to sharing his feelings.

On the plus side, ever since taking me to the theater, Jason had been less persistent in his pursuit of me. He'd apparently taken to heart my need for a stress-free friendship and hadn't once stepped over the line. He didn't try to hold my hand or kiss me again. Every now and then, I'd catch a glimpse of desire in his eyes, or perhaps it was longing, but he never acted on it. I was truly having a great time hanging out with Jason. He'd lived in Manhattan most of his life, but as he showed me his favorite sights around the city, he acted as if he was seeing everything for the first time. So he'd enticed me to take the Staten Island Ferry, spend hours in the Metropolitan Museum of Art, spend more hours exploring Little Italy and Chinatown and Central

Park. But no matter what we were doing, Jason always made me feel as if it was fun and special because he was with me. Jason behaved as if he couldn't imagine being anywhere else.

I knew Jason wanted more than friendship from me, but as much as I enjoyed being with him, I kept him at arm's length. I wasn't even sure why anymore. Jason was attractive, considerate, passionate, and interested in me. A man who talked about everything, his emotions, his life, my emotions, my life. How Jason enjoyed talking! I finally had a chance to have the type of relationship I needed. Jason was a great guy and I liked him. So, what was stopping me from taking the next step?

It couldn't be Hugh. I wouldn't let it be Hugh, a man who would scarcely admit to having emotions, let alone talk about them. I hadn't heard a word from him since he'd taken me to dinner and then expected me to go to bed with him. Hugh hadn't gotten what he'd wanted, so, naturally, he'd disappeared from my life.

Damn you, Hugh!

JOYCE COMPLAINED the entire time, constantly interrupting my performance. I knew Joyce was right about one thing: my portrayal of Edgar hadn't been at all convincing. What was wrong with me? Edgar was an intense man who attempted to manipulate Pete's and Lori's emotions out of loneliness, while still harboring a genuine need to seek their forgiveness and receive love. But whenever I spoke my lines, I couldn't seem to bring those complex qualities to life. My lunch as Edgar had done nothing to help me get a firm grasp on his true nature.

Predictably, this got Joyce going. She and Jason began arguing, which of course set Lindsey off, and it all went downhill from there. Hours of fighting. In total Lindsey fashion, she stomped off the stage. Joyce followed suit, leaving me and Jason alone onstage.

"What a complete waste of time." I wiped the perspiration from my forehead. "I don't know how we're ever going to pull this play off. We're only three actors and one director, but the politics involved are incredible."

"It's a good sign that things are going so badly."

I wasn't really in the mood to joke about it. "Let me guess," I said sourly. "Theater superstition has it that crummy rehearsals make for a glorious opening night?"

"No. But the way I look at it, things can't get much worse than this. And if things can't get worse, they have to get better."

I smiled. Jason had a habit of doing that—making me smile at his reasoning. Jason came around behind me and proceeded to massage my tense shoulders. Along with all his other positive qualities, Jason knew how to give an excellent shoulder massage.

"Where shall we eat tonight?" Jason asked.

"I don't know if I'm all that hungry." What I needed was a stiff drink and some downtime after the tension of the afternoon.

Jason turned me around. "Then let's go to my place. We can kick back, relax, and if you get hungry, I'll fix you something to eat."

"You cook too?" I asked in surprise.

"No, I said I'll *fix* you something, not cook it. I've got cold cuts for sandwiches or leftover pizza you can nuke."

"Figures," I chuckled. "But I don't know if it's such a good idea." I'd never been to Jason's apartment, and for some reason, it felt like I'd be crossing a line if I went.

"Ben, what are you afraid of?"

"I don't know."

He drew me close, and I could tell he wanted to kiss me, but Jason didn't act on that desire. Strangely enough, I was mildly disappointed when he pulled away and said, "C'mon, Ben, it'll be fun. We'll kick back, watch some TV, and just veg."

I was becoming quite the basket case, no longer sure what I wanted. Hugh was always skirting the edges of my thoughts. I couldn't seem to get rid of him. Maybe I hadn't truly tried to. I'd given my heart to a man who couldn't do the same for me. It was time I took it back. Hugh didn't deserve it. Maybe Jason did. Jason was certainly offering me his on a silver platter. Maybe it was time to move on.

I hesitated another long moment and then nodded slowly. "Yeah, I'll go home with you."

I SAT stiffly on the couch in Jason's apartment, feeling uncomfortable and ill at ease. I'd tried to convince myself it was time to move on, yet I'd brought Hugh along with me. Jason's place was nothing like Hugh's. Where Hugh's main homes were showy in an old-world style, Jason's was eclectic. The furniture was modern, made of chrome and glass, with pops of bright blues and yellows. Yet, there were wooden shelves filled with books, photos, random knickknacks that had no theme, no rhyme or reason, but the pieces fit together. The place was much like Jason's personality, fun and modern with an appreciation for the past.

"Nice place," I said at last, trying to sound nonchalant.

Jason brought two bottles of beer from the kitchen and handed me one before taking a seat on the coffee table. "Thanks. It's nothing fancy, but I like it."

"I'm not into fancy, so we're good."

"So it's not my decorating skills that has you tense. Must be me."

"No, it's not you. Rehearsal was horrible, and I can't help but think my first big shot at acting is never going to become reality." It wasn't a complete lie. I was worried about the play. Jason didn't need to know about what else was weighing heavily upon me. Jason rose to his feet, then took the seat next to me. He bumped his shoulder against me. "I promise the show will go on and you'll be fabulous."

"Well, at least one of us is confident."

"That's all it takes sometimes." Jason grabbed the remote from the side table and clicked on the TV. "What are you in the mood for? Sports, documentary, movie?"

"I'm not really into sports, but I wouldn't say no to a good comedy."

Jason sat back and ran his palm over his jaw. "A good comedy, huh?" He flicked through the channels, but after a moment he shrugged. "Sorry, all I can find is action/adventure, chick flicks, or horror."

I took a big pull from my beer, then yawned. "Actually, I'm pretty tired, and I'm thinking I need a hot bath and a pillow."

"But you just got here. I can order some pizza and a comedy."

"I don't know…."

"C'mon, Ben. You wanted me to back off and I did. I just really enjoy spending time with you."

"I know and I like hanging out with you, honestly I do."

"Then you'll stay?"

I yawned again, suddenly weary mentally and physically. I needed time to get my head on straight and figure out why I had told Jason to back off, then felt disappointed when he didn't kiss me. I really wasn't in any shape to be around anyone. I set my beer on the coffee table and went to my feet. "Can I get a rain check?"

Jason's face fell, his expressive face showing his disappointment. I almost sat back down, but I knew I couldn't. Jason got to his feet. "I'll walk you out."

"That's okay." I gave Jason a small hug, patting his back before stepping back and smiling. "I'll see you tomorrow."

"I'm going to hold you to that rain check."

I stopped at the door, hand on the knob, and looked back at him. "I hope you do." And I meant it. Jason was really trying, and I appreciated it. Maybe Jason and I could become great friends, and if more happened between us… well, I wasn't sure what to think about that. I headed home, feeling even more confused. I truly worried for my sanity.

CHAPTER FIFTEEN

I HATED the fact that I was quite possibly stringing Jason along, yet there was part of me that hoped once I got Hugh out of my head and reclaimed my heart, I'd feel the spark between Jason and me. Or maybe I was just a selfish son of a bitch. Either way, I'd suggested Jason have dinner at my place. Of course, I then was instantly guilty because he offered to cook. Still, I didn't say no. Yup, I'm totally a selfish son of a bitch.

I set the table, then went in to check on Jason's progress. The kitchen wasn't big enough for two to move around without bumping into each other, so I moved up behind him. I went on tiptoes and peeked over his shoulder. "That doesn't look or smell like spaghetti sauce from a jar."

Jason looked back at me with a sly grin. "Yeah, well, wait till you try it before getting too excited."

He dipped the wooden spoon into the sauce, blew on it, then brought it to my lips. I opened my mouth and was hit with an amazing flavor of tomatoes, oregano, and basil. "Damn, that is really good."

"You're just saying that."

"No, I'd tell you if it tasted like shit, trust me."

"There really is something to that beginner's luck thing, huh?" Jason asked.

I popped him on the arm playfully, then stepped back. "You're so full of it."

Jason just laughed.

I worked my way past him, grabbed the bottle of white wine I had chilling in the fridge, then headed back to the dining area, or the area we'd set up to eat. It was a card table and folding chairs, but it worked.

The sound of someone knocking on my door stopped me midstep. I wasn't expecting anyone. I glanced at Jason, then back toward the door. The knocking came again. I set the bottle of wine on the table. Curious, I walked to it, my hand on the lock. I didn't live in the best of neighborhoods. Then I chastised myself—like a robber would knock first. "Who is it?"

"Special delivery."

I glanced at Jason once again. What was he up to? I wouldn't put it past him to send me flowers or a singing telegram or something just as silly. I unbolted the locks and opened the door and got the shock of my life.

"Hugh! What in the hell?"

Hugh pushed past me with…. *What the hell?* He had a bicycle. I gawked at him, not too pleased to see him.

"Hugh, what are you doing here? What's this all about?" I eyed the bike suspiciously.

"We're going for a bike ride. Central Park," Hugh announced. He propped the bicycle up by its kickstand. "I have one just like it downstairs."

"Hugh…." I gritted my teeth. "Dammit, you can't just come charging in like this and expect me to…." I shook my head. "You just can't."

"Benny, I'm just asking you to come with me. A bike ride, nothing more. We'll spend the afternoon together. What do you say?"

"I can't."

"Why not?" Hugh moved closer to me, which wasn't very easy considering how much space the bike was taking up.

I stiffened, watching Hugh's response to the rustling sound from the kitchen. I knew the exact moment when Hugh spotted Jason. The muscles in Hugh's jaw twitched, and his eyes narrowed.

Great, just fucking great!

A flush moved up from Hugh's neck to his cheeks. His eyes went a little wild, and for a second, I feared Hugh was about to start a fight. The tension in the room grew painfully thick until I was practically choking on it.

I glanced back and forth between the two men, ready to step between them if the pissing contest started. It was Jason who made the first move. He walked over to my side without ever taking his gaze from Hugh. The expression on Jason's face could only be described as combative. Hugh glared back and I swear he puffed up a little to make himself appear more intimidating. Well, I don't know if Jason was, but I certainly was worried. Both of them were a lot bigger than I was. How in the hell would I pull them apart? If they started to go at it, I'd have no choice but to sit back and let them go.

Something changed in Hugh. Regret? Disappointment? I wasn't sure, but relief washed over me when Hugh blew out a heavy breath and said, "You're right, Ben. I can't just come charging in like this. I made a mistake."

I instantly felt guilty, which was ridiculous. Hugh was my ex. He'd shown up unannounced, and I didn't have to explain myself. "I... um...." I gestured with my free hand at the bicycle. "This is just a little overwhelming."

"Look, I'll have someone pick up the bike later when your elevator's working."

"You carried it all the way up here?" Which, duh, was a really stupid question. How else would he have gotten it up here?

He didn't answer my question. "Like I said, I'll have it picked up later." Then he left the apartment, closing the door after him.

I stood there dumbfounded, staring long after Hugh left. Just moments before, I would have sworn there wasn't a single romantic bone in Hugh's body. I ran my fingers over the petals of the bundle of daisies sitting in the wire basket. Hugh never bought me flowers unless he had his secretary send them on my birthday. And a bike ride in Central Park? Who was that guy and what had he done with my ex?

"That went well," Jason said from behind me.

I spun around and gawked at him. "I'd hate to see your idea of something that *didn't* go well."

"No one ended up in the hospital or jail, I'd say that was a win." A buzzer went off. "Oh, and look, dinner is done."

I followed Jason into the kitchen. "You know, you didn't have to antagonize him."

"I did no such thing," Jason said flippantly.

"Whatever! You knew that's exactly what you were doing when you moved up close to me like you were taking possession of me." I crossed my arms.

Jason didn't respond until he had two plates of spaghetti plated. "Hey, I was just following your lead. You told him he couldn't, and I was just making sure he didn't." He held up a plate. "Hungry?"

I was about to protest, wanting to talk about what just happened, but my stomach betrayed me by growling loudly. I huffed out a breath, then took the plate. I was glad someone found the situation funny because I sure as hell didn't.

I took my plate to the table. Jason took the other chair across from me. I didn't look up—he'd just crack some silly joke and make me smile. Jason had an annoyingly creative way of doing that. I swirled my fork in the noodles, picked up a good amount, and shoved it into my mouth.

It was delicious. At least something good had come out of the evening. I was going to need my energy to deal with the epic crap that had just landed in my lap. I stole a glance at the bike with a basket full of daisies. Christ, my life was fucking complicated.

CHAPTER SIXTEEN

JASON PLACED a ball of putty on his nose, then slowly began shaping it. I sat across from him, watching in a sort of unwilling fascination. Jason was making himself up for a benefit performance tonight. This was his third attempt at creating a new nose. Apparently, he was a perfectionist when it came to such matters.

I examined the trays of supplies on the counter. It wasn't as impressive as those given to the contestants on *Face Off*. Then again, Jason was turning himself into an old man, not a cosmic circus challenge. "How long have you been doing makeup?"

"Since before my first role when I was in first grade. I figured, when no one wants me to be an actor anymore, I can become a makeup artist." Jason, finally satisfied with the shape of his nose, proceeded to stipple the texture.

"I've noticed that acting doesn't seem to…. Well, I mean you don't seem to take it that seriously, and I think that's why you enjoy it so much."

"You don't sound like you're paying me a compliment," Jason remarked. "You sound like you're complaining."

"No, that's not it at all. I admire you for it. With me, I seem to take everything way too seriously. Acting in particular. The harder and harder I try to grasp Edgar's character, the more it escapes me. I'm really beginning to worry about it."

Jason had started in on the greasepaint, but he turned to look at me. The humped nose made him appear rather sagacious. "You're definitely not relaxing with the part," he said. "Maybe I'm imagining things, but you've been worse since the bicycle thing."

I wished he wouldn't keep referring to it that way, as "the bicycle thing." I wished Jason wouldn't refer to it at all, but he seemed to have a need to keep bringing it up.

110

"Jason, that was almost a week ago. I've tried to put it behind me. You should do the same."

"If you've put it behind you, then why is that bike still cluttering up your living room?"

"I'm sure Hugh will send someone to pick it up soon."

"You seem to like having it around," Jason persisted. He made the bike sound as if it was Hugh I was keeping in my apartment. Ha! Hugh living in my dive. That would be the day.

"The truth is, I'm hardly ever in my apartment," I said lightly. "If we're not rehearsing, you're always taking me off somewhere. Take tonight, for instance, the benefit where you'll be performing."

Jason picked up his greasepaint stick and tapped it against his palm. "Sounds like you're complaining again. Ever since the bicycle thing, you haven't seemed quite as happy with me."

"Jason, will you stop with the goddamn bicycle thing," I snapped.

"I know I promised to try and be your friend, but dammit, Ben, I love you."

Jason had never said it quite that way before. It had always been, *Ben, I think I'm falling in love with you.* This time, there were no qualifiers. It was a simple, clear-cut "I love you." He sat there with his putty nose, waiting for me to respond, and I couldn't.

"I wish I knew what it would take to get him out of your head," Jason said at last. "And I wish I knew what it would take to get that damn bike out of your living room."

I felt an ache inside, an ache that was becoming more and more familiar. "Maybe we just need to give it some time," I said quietly.

Jason frowned. "Are you going to tell me that we're rushing it? I haven't even tried to hold your hand or kiss you in weeks. If that's rushing it…."

Jason didn't need to finish the statement. I knew exactly what he meant. "Can we please not get into this right now?"

He seemed about to say something more but then went back to creating his new face. Jason shaded lines onto his forehead and cheeks with a brush, then used another along his jaw.

By now I was aware of all of Jason's good qualities. I enjoyed being with him, loved the way he could always make me smile even when I didn't feel like it. I had grown to genuinely care about Jason. So, why couldn't I take the next step? Jason obviously cared for me, so why was I holding back?

If I was being completely honest, that bicycle in my living room plagued me with other unanswered questions. Why had Hugh shown up so unexpectedly? What had he intended? Had he simply been trying another method to get me into bed? Except it didn't seem like Hugh's style. He wasn't one to use subterfuge. And those flowers… those flowers had seemed genuinely romantic. Flowers that, for some reason, I hadn't been able to take out of the wire basket. They were wilting there, dropping petals all over my floor.

And that brought me to another question. Why hadn't Hugh sent someone to pick up the bicycle as he'd promised? It almost seemed as if he was leaving it with me as some sort of reminder. A reminder of what? Perhaps none of those questions merited an answer. Whatever Hugh had intended that day, it was just too late to find out. Because I had gone on with my life. I was starting to get involved with another man. A man who loved me. Only one thing was lacking. I had to decide if I loved Jason back. When I did, well, everything would be settled.

Jason had finished his makeup job, and it was a bit startling. There were subtle grooves on his cheeks and across his forehead, and even more subtle shadowing along his jaw. It was the sort of face that would do very well for the part of the Edwardian gentleman Jason was playing tonight.

"Just think. You stick with me, Ben, and you could come home to someone different every night."

"No, thank you. I'll stick with the original."

"Do you mean that?" Jason was suddenly very serious.

"Of course, but if you think I'm going to fall at your feet and swear my eternal devotion, you've got another think coming, mister," I said in a light tone. I ruffled his hair playfully. "C'mon, let's see if you can impress me with your acting skills as much as you have with your makeup talents."

Jason stuck out his bottom lip in a mock pout, the slight smile curling his lip ruining the effect. I had no doubt that Jason would love for me to declare my undying love for him. The fact that he could still smile after he'd told me he loved me and I hadn't been able to do the same was even more impressive than the transformation he'd made in his appearance.

A short while later, we caught the subway uptown. Jason enjoyed sitting on the train in his high starched collar, homburg hat, and theatrical makeup, already in character as an Edwardian gentleman. But if he expected to draw stares or comments, I knew he was bound to be disappointed. The jaded New York commuters took him in stride.

We arrived at the Atwood, a beautiful old hotel with an ornate facade of Gothic arches. The place was equally gracious and ornate on the inside. Soon I was part of the audience in the large banquet room, watching the opening act on stage. Jason belonged to a troupe that periodically put on plays to benefit different charities. Tonight's performance was part of a fund-raiser for a medical research foundation. And it was a delightful performance—a farcical murder-mystery romance. Jason portrayed a very proper gentleman caught up in solving the crime.

He was a good actor, there was no denying. Jason seemed immersed in the role without letting it burden him, conveying the sense that he was quietly poking fun at the character he played. Such an attitude was perfect for tonight's comedy. I watched him with a mixture of envy and admiration.

I was a fortunate man, I told myself, to have Jason in my life. Yes. Very fortunate indeed.

I just had to keep telling myself that.

CHAPTER SEVENTEEN

I ARRIVED at work to find an honor bestowed on me. For the first time ever, I would be allowed to move up to cashier. Mel had been assigned to teach me the ropes. Only, if one of the requirements was to greet the customers with a smile, she failed miserably.

Mel's face looked drawn today, her movements too meticulous, too precise, as if she feared that at any moment something inside her might shatter. "Always count the money back to them," she said, a forced briskness in her voice. "And whatever you do, don't forget to ask if they would like their receipt." She nodded to the sign taped to the counter. It informed the customer that if we forgot, their next meal was free.

"What happens if I forget?" I asked.

"You know Geovanni." Mel's tone was mocking now. "He says that we all have to pay for our mistakes if we're to learn from them."

I glanced at her. Mel's face still had that pinched look, as if she was trying very hard to contain all her difficult emotions.

"How's it going?" I asked gently. "We've hardly had a chance to talk lately."

"Everything's fine," Mel said crisply. "Just fine."

"School going okay?"

"Of course school is going okay. And for your information, Ben, everything's fine with Toby too. That's what you really want to know about, isn't it? Whether or not I'm still seeing Toby. Well, I am seeing him. And everything's fine."

"Woah! Did I slap a sore spot or what?"

Mel glared at me, looking like a crazed woman. I was worried she was going to pounce at any moment. Then, just as quickly as her anger blew up, she seemed to run out of steam. For once, she didn't bustle about, trying to avoid me. She just stood there, both hands flat on the counter, staring down. "I've been late for class, ditching friends, and my grade in psych class is slipping," she whispered.

"Well, considering how well-endowed he is—"

"It's not funny," Mel snapped. "You don't know how hard I've worked to maintain my GPA. I could get kicked out of honors. And for what! A little dick?"

Ten inches was far from little, but I wasn't going to correct her. She was a mess. "I'm not making light of it," I assured her. "I didn't realize it had gotten so bad."

"I don't know how it happened. One minute I was on top of the world, I knew exactly where I was going and what I had to do to get there and then…."

"And then you fell in love," I finished for her.

Melanie snapped her head up and gawked at me. "Ben, I am not! I can't be in love. I just…. Dammit, what am I going to do?"

I patted Mel's back. "It's okay, Mel. We don't get to choose when our hearts take a leap. Is it really so bad to fall in love with someone?" A thought occurred to me. "Unless, he doesn't feel the same way. Is that why you're so sad?"

Mel shook her head. "I'm pretty sure he feels the same way even though I specifically told him our relationship couldn't be any more than physical. He just had to go and turn out to be smart and sexy and caring and just so, so… ugh, so fucking wonderful."

Mel sounded so miserable, poor thing. I wrapped my arms around her and hugged her. "So you just have to readjust your plan a little. I know you can do it. When you set your mind to something, you accomplish it."

"But—"

"But nothing." I grasped Mel's shoulders and held her an arm's length away until she met my gaze. "You can do this. The nice thing is, you'll have someone to stand with you, to support you while you're chasing your dream. A dream, from what you've told me, is Toby's too. So get there together. If you ask me, I'd say it's a lot easier to reach that goal with someone racing with you towards it."

Mel gave me a slight smile. "How did you get so smart?"

I kissed her forehead. "I'm not. You're the smart one. I just needed to remind you of that."

Mel threw her arms around me and hugged me tight. "Thank you."

"You're welcome." I patted her back. "Now get back to work before being in love is the least of your worries and paying your light bill will be."

AFTER THE conversation with Mel, I'd been thinking a lot about her situation. I remembered that first love, the excitement, the wonder. Everything but that person—in my case Hugh—consumed every thought. I wished I still felt that way. The naive belief that love could conquer everything and anything. Life had a way of jading someone after a while. It certainly had me. I hoped the best for her. Hell, she and Toby had something me and Hugh never had—a shared dream. The thought was sobering.

I was looking forward to rehearsing my lines with Jason. I needed something to take my mind off my own life. Diving into Edgar's was what I need. Only, Jason had other ideas.

"Marry me," he said.

I lowered the script and looked at Jason in confusion. "What? There are no marriage proposals in this play."

Jason tossed his own script aside and came to clasp my hands in his. "I know. This is me proposing to you. Marry me, Ben."

All I could do was stare at him in complete shock for several ticks of the clock. "You're not serious."

"Totally. Marry me, Ben."

I couldn't believe I'd heard him correctly. Jesus Christ, it had only been a few days since I told him I wanted a friend and acting partner, nothing more at the moment. Apparently, Jason hadn't heard a damn word I said. What was it about the men in my life that refused to listen to me? I tightened my hands around the script, anger flaring up in me. Fuck! I just wanted to rehearse our parts for the play, to immerse myself in the role of Edgar. Dammit, I didn't want to think about anything dealing with reality, and I certainly didn't want to ponder marriage.

Jason, however, was not going to let the matter rest. He sat down on the old-fashioned trunk across from me, looking very expectant.

"Are you out of your goddamn mind?"

"Perhaps. But give me three good reasons why you shouldn't marry me. No, make that five. Five good reasons."

"Why stop with five?" I asked, not even trying to hide my irritation.

If Jason noticed the daggers I was shooting out of my eyes at him, he didn't seem phased by them. "I do believe you just threw out a challenge. I accept."

"What the hell are you talking about?"

"You said why stop at five, I challenge you to come up with five. I bet you can't do it."

I narrowed my eyes. "Here's a suggestion. Let's just forget you asked and we'll get back to reading lines."

"Ben, I never pegged you for someone who walked away from a good honest challenge."

"Jason—"

"C'mon, humor me. Give me five reasons. That's all I'm asking. Just five reasons why we shouldn't get married."

He was impossible. I was either going to have to play Jason's little game before we could get any work done or I could take my script and go home.

I stared at Jason, who was looking at me with that damn confident smile, challenging me. Ugh! "Reason number one, we haven't known each other long enough."

"How long does it take?" Jason asked immediately. "I realized how I felt about you practically the first minute I met you. And you already know everything important there is to know about me."

I did know the most important thing about Jason. He wasn't afraid to share all his thoughts and feelings with me.

I held up a second finger. "Reason number two, I'm too old for you."

"Those nine years again? I thought we'd left that behind us?"

I ignored Jason's question and held up a third finger. "Reason number three, I have enough going on in my life right now without having to worry about a wedding."

"Marriage would actually simplify things between us. You could move in here with me."

"No," I said firmly. "It most certainly would not simplify things. Besides, your place is too small." I'd been down that road before. I would never start any future relationship on such uneven footings. It would be either in a home we purchased together or it wouldn't happen. End of story.

"So we get a bigger place together."

"No. I don't have time to move, and neither do you." I stood and crossed to one of the windows. It was dark outside, but I could see into the lighted windows of another apartment building across the street. I saw a man nestled into an armchair, reading. A man alone. It was a peaceful, refreshing sight. In that moment, I envied him.

"Reason number four," I said. "We don't even know if we're compatible in bed. That's like buying a pair of shoes without trying them on. Not going to happen."

"Well, you know I'm willing to let you try me on for size," Jason said, dropping his tone to a seductive level.

I ignored his comment. "And reason number five, I'm sorry, Jason, but I'm not a place in my life emotionally where I can commit to anyone. My head's all messed up, and that doesn't make for a real good start to a marriage."

"It's him, isn't it? Always the ex. Why did you leave him if you can't get him out of your mind?"

I swiveled around. "Believe it or not, what I'm talking about doesn't have anything to do with Hugh. It's about you and me." I paused, but I knew that eventually I had to bring it up. I wasn't doing either of us any favors by keeping my frustration to myself. "We have something we need to resolve," I went on. "Sometimes I feel a little crowded, Jason. I told you I need you as a friend and acting partner, but you ignored me or simply didn't hear me."

"I heard you, but you're not the only one in this relationship that has needs."

"You're right. That's why you shouldn't be chasing me. I'm not in a place in my life where I can give you what you need. I don't know if I ever will be, because I don't fucking know right now," I snapped.

"Come off it, Ben. If it weren't for Bayard, you wouldn't be telling me any of this. You're inventing excuses."

I huffed out an exasperated breath. "There you go again. You haven't heard a single thing I've said."

"I've heard," he muttered. "And I've observed a few things. Such as the fact that you still have a bike in your living room, dripping dead flowers all over the rug."

I couldn't deny the ever-intrusive fact of that bike. Just as I couldn't explain why I hadn't called Hugh and demanded that he have them removed from the premises. Nor could I explain why I hadn't tossed all of it out the window.

"Jason, leave Hugh out of this. You're missing the point. It wouldn't matter who I was involved with, I'd still want a certain amount of space." I didn't mention that between Hugh and me there'd been too much space. Was there no happy medium? With Hugh, I had known distance, and with Jason, I knew togetherness and then some. Was I asking too much from life, wanting just the right balance?

Jason stood. He stuffed his hands into his pockets, somehow managing to look both mournful and belligerent at the same time. "I wish I could knock the hell out of your ex. And I wish there was some way you could think about me, only me."

I realized Jason really hadn't heard a word I'd said. Perhaps his confused feelings concerning Hugh were a problem, but Jason and I had a problem entirely separate from that. Jason just couldn't seem to see it.

"Jason, you're so even tempered about acting. But when it comes to love—"

"When it comes to you, Ben," Jason said in a low voice, "I'm so in love I can't think straight."

Once again, I had no clue what to say. It seemed that was becoming a pattern in my life. The one thing I knew for sure was, Jason and I couldn't be friends. The realization caused my chest to tighten. I really did care about him—he was a great guy, but he was also in love with me. The second thing I knew for sure was, I could never love him the way he needed me to.

CHAPTER EIGHTEEN

ANOTHER CRAPPY day at work—rehearsal had been crap; my whole life seemed to be craptastic.

I lay in bed, singing a silly nursery rhyme in my head over and over to keep from thinking about anything remotely based in reality.

One, two, buckle my shoe.
Three, four, shut the door.
Five, six, pick up sticks.
Seven, eight, lay them straight.
Nine, ten, a big fat hen.

The telephone rang, interrupting my song.

Who would be calling at this hour? It was after midnight. I reached over and snatched my cell from the bedside table on the fourth ring.

"Hello," I said apprehensively.

"Benson! I'm so glad you're there. I simply didn't know where else to turn."

"Mother, what's wrong?"

"I know I'm calling too late. I'm sorry I disturbed you, dear. I just didn't know what else to do."

"Are you all right? Are the uncles all right?"

"Walter and Uncle Johnathan are fine."

"Mother, please don't keep me in suspense."

"I need you to come to Charleston tomorrow. It's rather urgent. And it's not really the type of thing I can explain over the phone."

I didn't like the way my mother sounded. There was an edge to her voice, as if she was just barely managing to keep herself under control.

"I think you'd better tell me what's wrong," I said firmly.

"Benson, please do this for me. Just come to Charleston. I can't face the situation alone."

"What situation?"

"I've arranged a flight for you. I will send your itinerary."

"Mother! Can you please at least tell me that you're well? I'll be worried sick thinking worst-case scenarios."

"Physically I'm fine, just please come. I need you here." She hung up before I could say another word.

I switched off my cell and set it on the table, my mind running a mile a minute. I'd have to turn my schedule completely upside down in order to travel to Charleston tomorrow. I'd miss work and rehearsal at a time I really couldn't afford to. Perhaps this was just another of my mother's schemes, or maybe she really needed help. Unfortunately, there was only one way to know for sure.

I WAS beyond irritated that once again I put my life on hold and rushed back home for one of Mary Grace's dramafests. I was sure that was exactly what was going on, considering that once I arrived, haggard and hungry, she'd refused to talk about anything until everyone was in attendance. She and her goddamn need to have an audience. The one highlight was getting to spend time with the uncles, who shared my frustration.

Walter and Uncle Johnathan anchored on either side of me, we walked along the path that led up to the back terrace of the Winthrop mansion, waiting to be summoned by Mary Grace.

"What in God's name has gotten into your mother this time, Benson?" asked Walter. "I have to admit, it's been rather peaceful since she's hidden herself away."

"You better not let Mary Grace hear you say that," Uncle Johnathan warned Walter from my left.

"Unlike you, I'm not the least bit intimidated by her. You really should try to get a backbone, Johnathan."

"Hmph, I have more nerve in my little finger than you have in your entire body," Uncle Johnathan countered. "And I most certainly am not intimidated by Mary Grace."

"Uh-huh." Walter sniffed. "Just the other day you went scurrying out of the room when you heard her heels clicking across the tile."

"I did no such thing!"

"All right, simmer down, you two," I said, barely able to contain my laughter. "There is nothing wrong with being a little nervous around my mother. Or at least being smart enough to avoid her at times."

Uncle Johnathan snorted. "Oh, how right you are, my boy."

"Well, we most certainly can agree on that," Walt added. "That's why you should come back to Charleston, Benson. The three of us could be a formidable force against our beloved matriarch."

"While that does indeed sound like a grand ol' time…." Uncle Johnathan gave in to a fit of laughter, the sound of which cause me to join in. I loved hearing him so happy. When he was in control again, he added, "Can you imagine what Mary Grace's perfectly sculpted hair would look like when we ganged up on her? She'd be pulling it out."

The idea sent us all into another fit of boisterous laughter.

It did my heart good to hear them laughing. After my last visit to Charleston, I'd been worried about them. They had seemed just a little more frail to me. Being with them now, I felt torn between my two lives as never before. I needed to be in New York. I needed the independence I'd found there. But I also felt the tug of loyalty toward my family. I realized that I missed these two exasperating dear men more than I'd been willing to admit.

"Care to share the joke?" asked a deep voice from the other side of the terrace. We stopped, then slowly I turned around to find Hugh coming toward us.

Walt, Uncle Johnathan, and I all looked at each other. Walt and I were still snickering. Uncle Johnathan gave a slight shake of his head, indicating we should keep our conspiracy against Mary Grace to ourselves.

"Just having a silly senior moment," said Walter, flashing a wide grin at Hugh. "But now that you're here, perhaps we'll find out what's going on. Why is Mary Grace in such a tizzy?"

"I'm afraid I don't know any more than you do. She's waiting for us in the dining room." Even as Hugh spoke, he continued to stare at me. I tried to be cool, indifferent, but I could feel my body heating.

"All you have to do is ask me what's going on and I'll tell you," Uncle Johnathan said.

Walter patted my arm. "Our poor Johnathan is slipping quickly into dementia today. He likes to think he knows everything that's going on, yet he can't even tell you what he had for breakfast."

"Oatmeal, toast, and juice," Uncle Johnathan said, sounding quite affronted.

As I propelled them forward a little at a time, Walter leaned in conspiratorially and whispered, "He had scrambled eggs."

I bit my bottom lip to keep from laughing. I was just glad Uncle Johnathan hadn't heard him. I could imagine the argument it would have produced.

We made our way into the house, Hugh going ahead to usher us through the archway and into the grand dining room. Mother sat at the opposite end of the impossibly long table. This room, like the ballroom, was one I especially disliked. The table could easily sit twenty, but oftentimes it was just me, Mother, and Father. Of course, we could have easily used the smaller nook in the kitchen, but Mother wouldn't hear of it, always having to put on airs even when alone with her family.

Mary Grace, looking unusually nervous, gestured for everyone to take a seat. I carefully helped Walter and Uncle Johnathan into chairs, then sat to the right of Mother. Hugh sat on the other side of the table, directly in my line of sight. He seemed to have no qualms about studying me. I frowned at him and tried to concentrate on the proceedings at hand.

Mary Grace folded her hands on the table but didn't speak. She seemed to be waiting for something. Maybe she was just trying to prolong the aura of suspense. If so, she was doing a good job of it.

Mary Grace continued to sit in silence at the head of the table, ignoring the uncles muttering to each other. There was a nervousness about Mary Grace I'd rarely seen. I had the impression that my mother might spring up and bolt from the room at any second. I glanced discreetly at Hugh. He sat there calmly, his face a mask of neutrality as he continued to stare at me. I felt as if I were some sort of weird bug under a microscope Hugh was trying to identify. I hated the feeling. I fidgeted in my seat, moving to the edge, ready to flee the moment Mary Grace did.

The door from the kitchen swung open and Charles—the ex-fiancé—appeared. He nodded to all present and moved to stand behind Mary Grace. Charles seemed perfectly collected. He'd always been a background sort of person, content to allow Mary Grace to take center stage. For years, he'd overseen a very successful real-estate business, but he'd recently taken early retirement to devote himself to a career as an amateur naturalist. The study of botany was Charles's greatest enjoyment, and I suspected he actually liked plants more than people.

"Thank you all for being here," Charles said. "As you may not be aware, Mary Grace and I have recently reopened discussions concerning our situation. Now we've reached a possible solution, but find it necessary to consult each of you regarding the matter. You, in particular, Hugh."

I looked around to gauge the reaction of Walter, Uncle Johnathan, and Hugh. There was none. Like this was completely normal. It struck me then how fitting this gathering was to the Winthrop tradition. Mary Grace and Charles, instead of solving their problems in private, had convened a family council. This always struck me as odd. The two of them discussing their affairs with the rest of the family sitting in like support staff. Not particularly conducive to romance.

My fidgeting increased, as did my anxiety, during the long, drawn-out pause. I frickin' hated these "family meetings." My ire at Mary Grace only grew. I huffed an exasperated breath, and Mother shot me a disapproving look. How dare I take the spotlight off her? Yeah, well, get on with it.

Finally, she took pity on us and spoke. "Charles and I have thoroughly discussed our situation. We agree that, if our marriage plans are to proceed, we must find a solution to our living accommodations."

Mary Grace paused. Her hands pressed tightly together, and she sounded even stiffer as she went on. "However, as Benson and Hugh once pointed out, perhaps it is advantageous for any marriage to start on neutral territory."

I studied my mother closely. Mary Grace didn't look too happy. How strange. It seemed a reconciliation was in the works, but my mother looked less than thrilled. It got me considering my situation with Hugh. Why did I want to be with him when half the time I was miserable thinking about him? I was beginning to suspect I was more like my mother than I was comfortable with. Before I had a chance to consider the frightening idea, Charles took up the topic again.

"Hugh, this is where you come in. Your parents' house has been vacant for some years, and if you were in the market to sell, Mary Grace and I would be interested in purchasing it. It would be the perfect solution to our current quandary. It would set Mary Grace's mind at ease being close to the uncles so she can oversee their care. Of course, the decision to sell is entirely yours. There is no pressure."

Hugh looked stunned. He ran his palm over his jaw, then rested his chin in his hand while he seemed to consider Charles's statement. After a moment he sat back in his chair and shrugged. "I'm not sure what to say. I hadn't really thought of selling the place. I'll have to think about it."

"Absolutely," Mary Grace said. "We want you to take all the time you need. There's no rush. And we want Uncle Johnathan and Uncle Walter to think the matter over. You, as well, Benson." Mary Grace stared anxiously at me. She almost seemed to be hoping that I would throw out some objection to the idea.

"Walt and I can take care of ourselves," Uncle Johnathan said. "Mary Grace, you should live wherever you please. Vienna, Brussels, or maybe you two should consider Zurich. It not only regularly tops Mercer's list, but others as well, as one of the best places in the world to live."

"What would you know of Zurich, Johnathan?" Walter asked in a scoffing tone. "Why should they move? I would think you'd want Mary Grace close by. Ben too. Life is too short to be without family."

"Walt, are you actually suggesting you care more about family than I do?"

"I said nothing of the sort. I was merely pointing out a fact. If it made you feel guilty, then perhaps you should take a look in the mirror."

"At least I can see my reflection, you old coot," Uncle Johnathan muttered beneath his breath. Dear Lord, how had these two stayed friends so long? Apparently it was their love for arguing as well as each other that was the recipe for success when it came to them.

The family meeting had disintegrated. The uncles continued to go at it, and Charles and Hugh moved to a corner of the dining room for their own discussion. I took advantage of the opportunity to grab my mother and ferry her down the hall to the sunroom. This was one of the least imposing rooms in the house and therefore my favorite. I gestured toward the wicker chaise longue. Mother took the seat, and I took the spot next to her.

"All right," I said. "Out with it. Why on earth have you let Charles talk you into this if it's not what you want?"

"Benson, whatever gives you the—"

"Cut the act, Mother. Out with it."

"First, Charles has not talked me into anything," Mary Grace insisted. "The idea is very sensible."

"What's wrong, Mother?"

Mary Grace leaned her head back on the chaise. "Is it so obvious that something's wrong?"

"You've gone to a great deal of effort to make it obvious, starting with your phone call last night. Apparently Charles isn't picking up on the clues, but I am."

Mary Grace sighed, without drama for once. "Benson, I'm so glad you came. I wonder if anyone else would understand what I'm going through." She straightened. "You see, I was so happy when Charles finally came to see me the other day. He'd put his silly pride away for once. How could it not mean a great deal to me?"

I refrained from mentioning that Mary Grace herself possessed a considerable amount of pride. Why hadn't she been the one to make the first move?

"Go on, Mother," I said patiently.

"Well, anyway, Charles came up with this idea about buying the Bayard house, and I let myself get swept along at first. I was just so relieved to have Charles back, I suppose I wasn't thinking very clearly. But now...."

"Is there something about that house you dislike?"

"No, no, of course not. Alex and Grace Bayard were dear friends of mine. It would almost be a way to honor them, making their home come to life again. Goodness knows Hugh hasn't been able to face the task."

"What is it, then?" I persisted.

Mary Grace suddenly looked despondent. "Benson... this isn't the easiest thing to confess, especially to one's own son. But I'm... afraid. Afraid of getting married again. Terrified, if you want to know the truth."

I reached out and patted her hand. I wasn't used to comforting my mother. "I had no idea."

"I have a confession to make. My hesitation has less to do with where we live and more to do with my fear of marrying again. I tried to ignore all the signs. Benson, your father and I had a very good marriage, but it wasn't perfect. Sometimes I needed more than he knew how to give. I never told you this because I wanted his memory to be special to you. I didn't want to ruin that."

I stared at my mother. "What was it he couldn't give you?"

Mary Grace smiled wistfully. "Haven't you guessed? It's the one thing you've always wanted from Hugh. A deeper love. A passion that goes to the soul."

Once again, I was forced to consider I had more in common with my mother. This time it wasn't quite as frightening. Maybe she did understand what I was going through with Hugh.

"I wish you'd told me about this a long time ago," I said softly.

"How could I? Don't you understand? I tried to hide it from myself. It's one thing to need a certain type of love, quite another to acknowledge it. And I was truly devastated when your father died. He was a good man. A man, in fact, very much like Charles. Dependable, kind… undemonstrative."

"I believe I am beginning to understand," I said. "You're afraid that your second marriage will be a repeat of the first."

Mary Grace made a small grimace. "It sounds so callous in a way, as if I'm somehow disparaging your father's memory."

"I know how much you loved him. Nothing can change that. But you've started to be honest with yourself, Mother. I don't think you can stop now."

"How can I want more than I already have? I've been a very fortunate woman. I was married to your father, and the Winthrop family accepted me as one of their own. Now Charles, a wonderful man, is willing to make compromises in order to marry me. And I have you, the great joy of my life! How can I possibly ask for more?"

I restrained my own rueful smile. Mary Grace was getting a little carried away again about the delights of motherhood. "Maybe it's not wrong to want more. Take it from me, the longing for the love you're talking about won't go away by itself. It's much better all around to deal with it."

Now Mary Grace was the one who patted my hand. "I so wanted Hugh to give you that type of love. I always believed, deep down, that he could give it to you."

"Mother, we need to talk about you," I said firmly. "There's only one solution. You have to go to Charles and tell him what the real problem is."

"I'm not ready for that yet."

"You'd better get ready, and soon. What if Hugh agrees to sell the house? You can't just go along with it."

Mary Grace jumped to her feet. "Benson, you must go talk to Hugh. Right now. Immediately. Tell him that he has to delay his decision as long as possible."

"This is ridiculous," I protested. "Talking to Hugh isn't the solution. Talking to Charles is."

"Benson, please. Do this for me. No need to tell Hugh all the details. Just ask him to wait before he makes up his mind. And then I'll be able to think about the rest of it."

I would have protested further, but I believed I understood my mother's turmoil. It was scary, all right, contemplating the idea of telling a man exactly what you needed from him. You could very well find out, once and for all, that he couldn't give it to you. That had happened to me with Hugh. He couldn't give me what I needed, and it still hurt. It hurt even after all this time.

I stood up and gave my mother a kiss. "I'll go talk to Hugh for you. As long as you admit that what you really need to do is to sit down with Charles for a heart-to-heart."

"I think I've admitted quite enough for one day," Mary Grace said, recovering some of her haughty airs. "Go, Benson."

And so I, the dutiful son, went to find my ex.

I went up the curved drive of the Bayard home and climbed the steps to the front door. I hesitated, debating whether to knock. The door was unlocked, and in the end, I simply went in.

I glanced first into one room, then another. Drop cloths covered the furniture. So many shrouded forms. It was sad. That was how this house had always felt to me, as if a sadness were trapped inside, like a ghost that couldn't escape.

I found Hugh in the main room. He stood motionless, gazing at the portrait of his parents that hung in a dim alcove. He didn't turn or acknowledge my presence. At last I came to stand beside him, and I too gazed at the portrait of his parents. Alexander and Grace Bayard, captured forever on canvas, were looking into each other's eyes so devotedly.

"They were very much in love, weren't they?" I murmured.

"Do you really think that?" Hugh asked, and the harshness in his voice startled me.

"Yes," I answered. "I know I was only a child when your father died, but I remember him and your mother together. And my own mother used to tell me stories about them, the perfect couple." Only now did I understand why sometimes Mary Grace had almost sounded envious recounting those stories. Perhaps Mary Grace saw in the Bayards' devotion to each other what had been missing in her own marriage.

"How little you know of the reality," Hugh said, his voice still harsh. "It's always been like you, Ben, to cast a romantic glow on everything. It prevents you from seeing what's really there."

Something in his tone was unfamiliar. It took me a moment to identify it as anger. Hugh was notoriously self-contained. Now he paced the room restlessly. "I can't understand why your mother and Charles want to live here. There are too many damn memories."

"Perhaps for you," I said carefully. "Charles, I'm sure, merely sees it as a convenient solution to his problems. As for my mother, the truth is, she's not really sure she wants to live here at all. She sent me with a message. She'd like you to wait on your decision until she really has time to think it through."

He looked irritated. "Maybe I'm missing something. In one breath she announces she wants to buy this house. In the next she announces she doesn't?"

"Something like that. It's a long story."

Hugh continued to pace. He was worked up in a way I had never witnessed before. One set of curtains in the room was partially open, but that didn't dispel the murkiness here. I shivered a little, even though I wasn't cold, and went to open the curtains farther.

"Don't do that," Hugh said, and now I heard a hint of pain in his voice. Just a hint, but it was there. I remained by the window, very still.

"Hugh, what did you mean when you said I knew so little of the reality? Tell me."

"Some stories shouldn't be told."

"No. You're wrong about that. Today my mother shared some things I wish I'd known years ago. But she's been smothering her emotions. It wasn't until now that they finally came out. I think you smother your emotions too."

"Leave it alone, Benny." His voice was rough.

I crossed to him and placed a hand on his arm. I could feel his muscles tense. "Something's going on," I said. "It's something to do with this house, isn't it? But what is it, Hugh? Don't shut me out this time. Please don't shut me out." I'd pleaded with him many other times, and it hadn't been any use. Hugh had always closed himself off from me. I hadn't been allowed to share whatever pain or sorrow Hugh had suffered in the past. Why should today be any different?

His silence defeated me. I dropped my hand from his arm and turned away. It was then that he spoke, and the pain in his voice deepened.

"Lord, Benny, I hate this house. I hate it. Yet I've never let go. Maybe I can't. That's the worst of it—maybe I just can't let go."

The shadows in the room thickened, the draped furniture looming eerily here and there, like so many shipwrecks in a mist. Hugh stood with his head bowed.

"The perfect couple," he said, his voice grating. "Yes, my parents could be the perfect couple when it suited them, when they wanted to put up a front. But here in this house, things were different. No pretense. They argued a lot. They tried to hurt each other. They knew how to do it too. After years of marriage, they understood each other's weaknesses."

I touched his arm again. "Hugh, I had no idea. I'm sorry."

"Don't be. I found a solution. I just got the hell out of here whenever I could. I probably spent more time at the office than my father did." Hugh pulled away and resumed his pacing.

"You know what's funny?" he said after a moment. "The worst times weren't my parents' arguments. The worst were the reconciliations. For a while, everything would be fine. They'd be enthralled with each other, as if they were trying to make up for all the hurt they'd inflicted. But I always knew that would change sooner or later. Another confrontation. Accusations, recriminations. More accusations… my mother's tears."

Hugh returned to the portrait of his parents. A veil of shadows and dust obscured it. "A good likeness," he said sardonically. "The way they're looking only at each other. Even when they were fighting and lashing out, they were absorbed in each other. I felt like an outsider most of the time. An outsider who didn't want to be anywhere near either one of them."

"Hugh, when your father died—"

"Enough, Ben." The warning was clear, but I didn't heed it.

"There's more, isn't there? I know there is. You have to talk about it."

"No." Hugh uttered only that one word, but I heard the heaviness in his voice. He bowed his head again in the gathering night.

I went to him then. This time I was determined Hugh wouldn't pull away from me. I wrapped my arms around him and held on to him as tightly as I could.

Hugh remained, head still bowed. But he didn't lift his own arms to hold me in return. It would be futile to push Hugh further— he'd shut down. His parents' relationship obviously was a sore spot, one that had festered for years and years. I couldn't help but wonder if it was the root of Hugh's inability to share his feelings. Actually, I was sure it was. However, until Hugh dealt with it, allowed the wound to heal, there was no hope for us. I laid my check against his chest, listening to the steady beat of his heart, wishing he'd allow me to help him mend it.

CHAPTER NINETEEN

SUNLIGHT GLINTED on the water, as Hugh stood at the helm of the boat. I welcomed the ocean breeze. I'd forgotten how good it felt to be out here like this. A little sailing seemed to be just what we needed. Amazingly Hugh had convinced me to come along. It had taken some doing, but he'd persuaded me.

I watched Hugh appreciatively. He hadn't lost any of his skill. He was expertly tending the jib sheets, allowing the boat to work with the wind and glide smoothly through the water. I tucked my hair back behind my ears, but the strands still came loose to whip around my face. I really needed a haircut. There were a lot of things I needed lately, especially finding some answers to all those damn questions.

A dazzling sky arching overhead, the cobalt ocean spreading out before us. It was precisely the atmosphere needed to set aside the past, the questions, the future, the pain, and just enjoy the here and now.

"How's it going in New York?" Hugh asked.

"Just fine." My voice sounded a little too clipped.

"Look," Hugh began, sounding awkward, "that time I showed up with the bike—"

"It was a nice idea. Just bad timing," I said.

"Are you serious about this Jason Collins?"

I yanked the jib, bringing it in too tight. Quickly I corrected it, then glanced at Hugh again. "Jason's asked me to marry him. I guess that means it's serious."

I watched Hugh's face carefully, but it was neutral. He gave nothing away as to how my declaration affected him.

"Set the date yet?" he asked nonchalantly.

And that just irritated the hell out of me. "For crying out loud, no! Of course I haven't. Do you honestly think I'd jump into another relationship just like that?"

"I don't know what you'd do, Ben. I've never quite figured you out. You're thinking about marrying this guy, aren't you?"

I sighed. "Jason is very nice."

"But that's not what I asked."

"Hugh, do you really want to get into it?" I certainly didn't. Why couldn't we just enjoy the beautiful sunshine?

"It's as good a subject as any."

"Well, I don't want to get into it. All I know is that I should have left for New York this morning. Yet here I am."

"Maybe I already know the answer. If you were going to marry him, you wouldn't be here with me."

"And maybe I shouldn't be. Every time I try to have a conversation with you, I end up getting agitated and just… just… I don't know, sad."

Hugh stared off into the distance. I began to wonder if he was going to say anything. He surprised me when he said, "I've never meant to make you sad. I've only ever wanted you to be happy." Hugh shook his head, looking truly miserable. "Collins, I suppose, doesn't make you feel like that."

"He irritates me sometimes, but no, he doesn't make me as sad as you do."

Hugh tied off the helm and came to sit next to me. He pressed his palm to my cheek, holding my gaze, his expression unexpectedly somber. He leaned in as if he were going to kiss me.

I jumped up, moved away from him.

"Benny—"

I turned to face him. "Sex won't solve anything. It's merely a reprieve from reality for a short time. It doesn't fix anything."

"I wasn't trying to seduce you."

"What are you trying to do?"

"I just want to be with you."

"Another way of saying you want to get me into bed."

Hugh shook his head vigorously. "No. I think about you a lot, and you may be quite surprised to know it's rarely about sex."

"Really?" I asked, skeptical.

"Yes, really," Hugh insisted. "I always wonder what you're doing, if you're with Collins. I mean, you have a new career, a new man, everything in place. I know I'm supposed to be happy for you. Hell, I should congratulate you for reaching your goal, but...."

I gawked at him. I didn't know this man before me. Twice now he'd shared his private feelings. I didn't move, didn't say a word for fear I'd wake up in my bed and it was all just a dream. But of course, Hugh left me hanging. My first instinct was to rant and rave, but it dawned on me how hard, how foreign this must be for him.

"These are the kinds of things I need to hear," I said gently. "Last night, when you were talking about your parents, I was beyond elated. You were actually sharing something with me, something real."

"I don't like talking about such things."

"Why does it scare you so much? Why is it so hard for you to expose your emotions to me? It's okay to be a little vulnerable."

"Vulnerable is just another way of saying weak," Hugh countered, sounding miserable.

I went and sat next to him. I wanted to pull him into a hug, tell him it was okay, but I didn't. Until Hugh dealt with the anger he was holding on to from his past, then it would never be okay. I caressed his back. "No, Hugh. It makes you human."

He didn't say anything else. After a few moments, he stood and got the boat headed back toward the docks. I watched the waves slap against the boat, and in the distance a gull cried. I was disappointed he had effectively ended the conversation, but I was thankful there had even been one. That glimmer of hope sparked again.

I prayed this time I wouldn't regret it.

I HONKED as the line of cars in front of me slowed. Not that it would do me any good. The stream of traffic was endless. It had been like this almost the entire way from Charleston.

"Benson, dear," said my mother from the back seat, "it really isn't polite to honk."

"Mother, do I have to remind you that I am not your chauffeur."

136

"That's quite obvious. I'd never hire you. You're much too aggressive of a driver."

"And your son."

"Yes, yes." Mary Grace waved a dismissive hand. "Hugh, please tell me you don't let Ben drive. He's really not very good at it."

"Luckily, they don't do much driving in New York City," said Hugh from the passenger seat.

I frowned. Hugh's presence was an unwelcome distraction. His presence, in fact, had been a distraction all day. Since we'd returned from sailing I kept waiting for him to say something. I was becoming impatient, which was ridiculous. I'd waited more than ten years for Hugh to open up to me, and now that he was beginning to, it was completely unrealistic to think he'd share in the course of one day everything he was feeling or had ever felt.

I honked again, loudly and deliberately, as the traffic came to a complete standstill.

"Really, Benson. You almost ran into that man's bumper."

"Mother!"

"It looked awfully close to me. What do you think, Hugh?"

"Let's just hope there was no exchange of paint," he said with a grin.

It was never Hugh's way to be tactful. With the vehicle stopped, I found my glance straying to him. He gazed back at me, and his eyes seemed particularly dark. What was he thinking? And why did he have to look so stubborn and attractive all at once?

"Benson, dear, I believe that now certain motorists are honking at you," Mary Grace said.

The traffic was moving again, and I pressed my foot on the gas. The car jolted forward, none too smoothly. Proof my mother brought out the worst in me, in more ways than one.

"I can't stop wondering what this is all about," Mary Grace said. "Charles made it sound so urgent."

"And why did he want Hugh and me to come too?" I asked.

"I have no idea. But you might want to move into the other lane."

I glared at my mother through the rearview mirror. "Would you like to drive? I'd be more than happy to let you." I held up my hands.

"Benson! You're going to kill us all."

"We're going five miles an hour, I'm quite sure you'd survive," I assured her.

"Hugh, would you please talk to him," Mary Grace pleaded. "I swear, I'm so tense I may just faint.

"I should get so lucky," I muttered.

"What was that?" Mother asked. Hugh on the other hand heard me and covered his mouth to hide his grin.

"Just complaining to the driver in front of me," I fibbed.

"You do realize they can't hear you?" Mother said sounding exasperated. I didn't respond. I didn't have to—Mary Grace had turned her attention from my driving on to Hugh.

"Hugh, dear. You don't have to make any quick decisions about selling your home. Take all the time you need. Charles and I have a great deal more to resolve than the simple matter of living accommodations."

"Uh-oh. Have negotiations crumbled?" Hugh asked.

"We've moved past that for the time being. Last night, at Benson's urging, I told Charles I wished to be swept off by him. Swept off, so to speak, on a white stallion." Mary Grace paused dramatically.

"A white stallion," Hugh echoed.

"You get the idea," I said.

"Oh. Romance, got it," Hugh answered doubtfully.

I tried to ignore him. "Mother, what did Charles have to say to all this?"

Mary Grace sighed. "Absolutely nothing. He just looked a bit panicked, told me I had a piece of leaf debris in my hair. And then he left."

My heart ached for her. I knew all too well what it was like to share your feelings with someone, only to have that someone ignore you. I cast a sidelong glance at Hugh. How all too well I knew. "Well, he did call you today. That's an encouraging sign."

"I'm not at all sure that it is." Mary Grace sniffed. "I wish he would have shared his intentions with me. I don't like surprises."

"Wait, I'm confused," Hugh said. "You want romance but don't like surprises? How can you have one without the other?"

"Not necessarily," I piped in before Mother could answer. "Sometimes the most romantic thing someone can do for you is simply be there. Listen. Touch. Share their heart."

"I take it this Collins guy does all those things?" Hugh asked, sounding slightly annoyed.

"Actually, he does. But we're not discussing Jason. Or romance or any of it—"

"You're the one who brought up the subject of romance," Hugh pointed out. "I'm just trying to learn a little about it."

"I most certainly did not. Mother did. How about we keep the focus on her?"

"You really should listen, Benson. Hugh says he wishes to learn."

"I doubt he's serious, Mother."

"Why? Don't you believe I'm capable of any romance, Benny?"

My gaze strayed to him again. Was that amusement I saw in his eyes? Or was he serious? That bicycle he'd hauled up to my apartment—that had certainly been a surprise. But romantic, I couldn't say. With Hugh, who could?

I wasn't sure how to answer Hugh's question. I honestly didn't know if he was capable of romance. Well, I supposed everyone could do something one would consider romantic, but without emotion, it really was a hollow gesture. Luckily, I would have more time to consider it because we'd arrived at the airport.

I pulled onto the tarmac as per Charles's instructions. And there was Charles himself, coming to open Mary Grace's door with a flourish. He assisted her from the car.

"Madam," he said, "your white steed awaits."

Technically, it may not have been a white steed, but it was a white plane—close enough.

I stepped from the car, coming around to stand next to Hugh. Mother looked shocked. "What in heaven's name have you done, Charles?"

"I have decided the particulars of our union can be worked out later. The most important thing is that you become my wife."

"Now?" Mary Grace squeaked.

"Yes, as soon as we touch down in Vegas. I've arranged everything."

Christ, no wonder Mother was so surprised—hell, *I* was surprised. It wasn't every day that your ex-fiancé whisked you into a chartered jet and flew you off to get married, just like that. It was certainly a surprise. It was *certainly* romantic. I couldn't deny either.

Now Mary Grace stood at the altar of the small wedding chapel, Charles by her side. Of course, the wedding chapel wasn't to Mother's taste. It was done up entirely in pink—pink walls, pink chairs, pink carpet. Even the flowers massed everywhere were pink. I thought it looked like some giant had spewed Pepto-Bismol.

As son of honor—stupid title—I stood beside my mother. Hugh, the best man, stood beside Charles. Filling the chairs behind us were many of Charles's and Mary Grace's friends. His chartered jet had taken on quite a load of passengers, including almost everyone they knew from Charleston. When Charles decided to do something romantic, well, apparently, he went all the way.

"Do you, Charles Henry Egan, take Mary Grace Winthrop to be your lawfully wedded wife, to have and to hold, to love and to cherish all the days of your life?"

"I do," said Charles. He was starting to look dazed, as if the magnitude of this adventure was only now starting to sink in.

"Do you, Mary Grace Winthrop, take Charles Henry Egan to be your lawfully wedded husband, to have and to hold, to love and to cherish all the days of your life?"

Mary Grace seemed incapable of speech. She just stood there, an awestruck expression on her face. The silence was starting to become noticeable. I wanted to offer her moral support but couldn't think of a discreet way to do it. I ended up giving her a nudge, and that seemed to do the job.

"Oh! Yes… yes, of course. I mean… I do!"

"I pronounce you husband and wife. You may now kiss the bride," said the officiant.

Charles embraced his wife, as pink helium-filled balloons were released into the air. Then the newly married couple went down the aisle, arms linked. Hugh and I followed, our arms not linked. The wedding guests trooped after us.

Charles had rented practically the entire hotel where the chapel was located. Everyone congregated in the ballroom, and the band struck up a waltz. Charles escorted his new bride onto the floor, Mary Grace still looking a bit stunned. She'd asked for romance and perhaps received more than she'd bargained for.

I sank down at one of the tables, frowning at the pink napkins, the pink mints, and the pink crepe-paper streamers.

"What's wrong, Benny?" Hugh asked as he pulled out a chair beside me. "This is supposed to be a celebration. Aren't you happy about it?"

I chewed one of the pink mints. It tasted like chalk. "Of course I'm happy. As long as my mother is happy."

"You don't look happy."

"You know, there are lots of appealing people here. Don't let me slow you down."

"I can't neglect my duties," Hugh said. "I'm the best man, remember? That means supervising the rest of the wedding party."

"Supervise somewhere else." I propped my chin in my hand, unable to explain the melancholy drifting over me. Maybe weddings always made me feel that way. They were occasions where so much was promised, so much expected of the future. But could the future ever live up to all the hype?

"Perhaps if you get your feet moving, your mind will follow." Hugh pulled me to my feet and out onto the floor. Another song had started, and several couples were dancing. Hugh pulled me close. I knew I ought to resist him. Certainly, I ought to resist the romantic music, tinged with its own sweet melancholy. But then I found my hands moving up over his shoulders. I pressed my cheek against Hugh's.

Being in his arms brought magic. It also brought torment because I would always require more than Hugh could give me.

Hugh knew how to hold ne when we danced—just as he did when we made love. But why didn't he know how to do it at other times? Last night, at his parents' house, he hadn't been able to hold me. I closed my eyes, wishing I didn't feel that ache inside, an ache of desire and disappointment that only Hugh seemed able to inspire in me. But I didn't let go of him. I just twined my fingers in his hair and went on dancing, wishing the music could go on forever.

The song ended, of course, the rhythm dying down. I clung to Hugh just another moment.

"You two certainly seem to be having a good time" came the cheery voice of Mary Grace Winthrop Egan.

With a start, I opened my eyes and pulled away from Hugh. Mother seemed to be making a recovery. She no longer looked dazed. She looked… sparkly. There was no other word for it.

"Excuse me, Hugh, while I borrow my son for a moment." Mary Grace propelled me off a little way, leaving Hugh to talk with the groom.

"Mother, is everything going all right? Is this what you wanted?"

"Goodness, dear, Charles could not have done a better job of sweeping me off my feet! I never imagined he had it in him. Not that it's easy for him either, you know. He'd much rather be in his gardens. The fact that he would do all this for me…." Mary Grace gave a tender little smile. "Well, I have my answer, Benson. Even when Charles decides to lose himself for hours in his greenhouse, I'll never again doubt his love for me."

"I'm glad for you, Mother. Very glad."

Mary Grace gave me a quick hug. "You were right all along, dear. I just had to ask Charles for what I needed. Now if only you and Hugh—"

"Mother, it's not always that simple."

"Isn't it, dear?"

"No, Mother, I'm sorry to say it isn't. Sometimes you ask for what you need and the other person just can't come through for you."

Mary Grace seemed ready to protest, but it was time for the toasts. As best man, Hugh raised the first glass.

"To Mary Grace and Charles. May their lives together always be filled with… surprises."

No one could accuse Hugh of wasting words. He looked right at me as he spoke, his expression seeming to carry some sort of challenge. I turned away from him and picked up my own glass of champagne.

Unfortunately, the rest of the toasts weren't as concise as Hugh's. They became progressively more long-winded and silly. The bridal couple began sneaking toward the door.

"Wait!" someone exclaimed. "What about the bouquet? You can't leave without throwing the bouquet!"

Mary Grace glanced down at the cluster of begonias and dahlias still clutched in her hand. She gazed around the ballroom, drew her arm back. After a moment of hesitation, she walked over and handed me the bouquet.

CHAPTER TWENTY

I AWOKE to the smell of warm flesh and stale champagne. I yawned, then winced at the pounding in my head. I tried to convince myself I was dreaming. It had to be a dream. The gust of snoring close to my ear, the masculine hand resting possessively on my thigh.... I sat up straight, and my head pounded all the more. Holy shit, I'd had this dream before. My heart seemed to beat in a tempo to match that in my head. A sense of foreboding engulfed me. What had I done? Oh, for fuck's sake, what had I done?

I stared at the sleeping form next to me. Hugh, hair rumpled on the pillow, snored in that restless manner of his.

A sense of dread growing, I glanced around the room. What I saw wasn't reassuring—the nearly empty bottle of champagne on the heart-shaped nightstand, the bouquet of begonias and dahlias tossed onto the floor, the discarded clothes strewn everywhere, the flocked wallpaper with its pattern of hearts.

Stomach clenched in dismay, I scrambled out of the bed. I grabbed my crumpled clothes, then hurried into the adjoining bathroom. I examined the place a bit wildly. Heart-shaped soaps, heart-shaped mirrors. Even the damn sinks were heart shaped.

I splashed cold water onto my face, hoping it would wake me from my nightmare. It did no good. I tried to put on my clothes, but somehow my briefs had become entangled in Hugh's boxers. Fuck! I finally managed to yank on my clothes, then sat on the edge of the tub and instructed myself on how to breathe. It had to be a dream. *C'mon, man! Please let it be a dream.*

Once again, I'd overindulged in alcohol—champagne this time. So had Hugh. That part I was willing to admit. But the rest of it—surely it couldn't really have happened. Hugh couldn't really have swept me off my feet and taken me into the wedding chapel. And the tall lady in pink surely hadn't performed another ceremony. *Do you, Benson, take Hugh....*

I moaned, got to my feet, my legs trembling, and went to stare at my ex, who was still slumbering. Except that maybe he was no longer my ex. Maybe I really had done the unthinkable. Maybe I'd actually married him!

I gazed at Hugh a moment longer, with all the heartache and longing and confusion inside me. Then I grabbed my shoes from the floor, took one more glance at Hugh, and fled.

Whether it was a dream or not, I planned on fixing it. I was going back to New York and carrying on with my plans as if this night had never happened.

"Wrong," said Joyce in a weary tone. "All wrong."

I gritted my teeth.

"Joyce," Jason put in, "Ben and I are going to take five. You don't mind?"

"Of course I don't mind. Why would I mind? Just because we're opening a week from tonight and nobody has a damn clue about what we're doing here—"

Lindsey slapped down her script. "I've had it. This time I've really had it."

Jason took me off to one of the small dressing rooms, where mildew spotted the walls and a dead cockroach lay feet up in the corner. The atmosphere fitted my mood, so I didn't protest. Jason closed the door, sat me down on a bench, and then stood back to survey me.

"Mind telling me what's going on? You've been avoiding me ever since you came back from visiting your mother two days ago. You won't go out to eat with me, you'll barely answer my phone calls, and during rehearsal, you won't even look at me. Ben, please tell me what's wrong?"

I had been waiting for just the right opportunity to tell him my problem—that I'd flown to Las Vegas, had too much champagne, and then married my ex. I really did want to tell Jason about all that, but somehow the right opportunity hadn't presented itself. This certainly wasn't it.

"Look, Jason, after rehearsal, we'll talk. Not now."

"When a man tells you 'not now,' you know you're definitely in trouble."

"Put a lid on it."

He looked injured. "You won't even let me come near you. What have I done?"

"It's nothing to do with you. It's just… I've made a monumental mess of my life, and I have no one to blame but myself."

I still couldn't believe I'd done it. What had possessed me? I couldn't just blame the champagne. Some craziness in me had taken over, and I'd done absolutely the worst thing possible. I'd committed myself to Hugh Bayard for the second time around.

I couldn't stop myself from leaning against the makeup table and burying my head in my arms. If this action bore any similarity to an ostrich burying its head in the sand, I chose to ignore the fact. I'd been so overwrought since returning to New York, I'd barely rested at all. I hadn't eaten much either, what with my stomach being clenched all the time. Somehow it didn't help matters that my *new* husband had made no effort to contact me during the past few days. The last time I'd seen Hugh, he'd been snoring in a rumpled Las Vegas hotel bed. I had caught a commercial flight back east, rather than face him again. I had inflicted the worst sort of pain and humiliation on myself by marrying him. But it hurt all the more, knowing that Hugh hadn't made even one effort to contact me. Never mind that I had made no effort to contact him.

Jason stroked my hair in a comforting manner. "You know you can tell me anything, don't you? Whatever's wrong, I'll understand."

Jason's understanding was going to be just a little stretched by what I had to tell him. I straightened and did my best to compose myself.

"Jason, I will tell you about it. But first we have to go out there and rehearse, try to pull this play together somehow."

146

Jason didn't look convinced, but he went out onstage with me. We ran through a scene with Lindsey/Lori. It went fairly well, although Joyce still complained about my interpretation. I just wanted the wretched rehearsal to be over.

At last it was. Jason and I were left alone, but that of course only presented me with another difficult situation. How did I tell Jason? How did I explain something I couldn't possibly understand myself?

We stood on the stage, facing each other, the stifling heat of the footlights upon us. I blotted the perspiration from my forehead.

"Jason… I'm sorry—"

"Maybe you shouldn't tell me," Jason said abruptly. "Maybe this is something I don't want to hear."

"I wish I didn't have to say it—"

"No, Ben." He stepped toward me, just as he had when we'd rehearsed our scene. He looked worried and suddenly quite a bit younger than his twenty-six years. "Don't tell me. For just a little while, let things be the way they were before. Just pretend that everything is perfect."

"Jason, it never was perfect for us," I said gently. "You know that. I wish it had been, though. I wish somehow it could have worked out."

Every emotion always showed on Jason's face. It was one of the reasons he was such a good actor—his ability to express the nuances of emotion even without words. And right now, what he was feeling was painfully clear to me. I saw the hurt I'd inflicted on him.

When he took a step closer and kissed me, I didn't pull away. It was a kiss of farewell. I knew it, and surely Jason did too.

"Still rehearsing? Or is this the real thing?" came a voice from beyond the footlights. Hugh.

I twisted from Jason's arms with a gasp as Hugh strode to the bottom of the steps leading up to the stage. He stopped there. Even though I was looking down at him, he seemed the one in command at the moment: hands in the pockets of his elegant trousers, the sleeves of his shirt rolled halfway up his forearms—effortlessly in command, that was the impression he gave. His face certainly betrayed no emotion beyond amused interest. If the line of his jaw looked a little tense and if that was storminess I detected in his dark eyes, well, maybe I was just imagining them.

I curled my hands into fists. I almost would have preferred Hugh to come barging onto the stage, claiming his husband from all usurpers. What would it take to really shatter his control?

I wasn't sure of my own control. My pulse had quickened the moment I'd heard Hugh's voice. It took everything I had just to gaze coolly back at him. "How long have you been here?"

"Long enough," Hugh remarked. "And it seems to me you're playing two fields, Ben. It could get a little wearing for you."

"I'm not playing at anything," I said sharply. "And I was just about to inform Jason of our… episode in Las Vegas."

"So that's what they call it nowadays. Times have changed since our first go-round."

"Las Vegas," said Jason. "What's this about Las Vegas?" He glanced from me to Hugh, then back to me. Now his expression was belligerent.

I took a deep breath. "Jason, the fact is…" I took another deep breath. "Hugh and I got married a couple of days ago." There. At last, it was out.

Jason's face registered shock and anger in quick succession. "Married? What the…?" He shook his head. "No. This has to be some kind of joke."

Seeing his anger was almost a relief. "Believe me," I said, "this isn't something I expected to do. It just… happened."

"That's right," Hugh said. "It happened. So now you can leave, Collins."

Jason stared at me for a long moment as if still hoping it was a joke. I didn't know what to say to him. Maybe there was simply nothing more to be said. At last Jason turned. He stomped down the steps, brushed past Hugh without looking at him, stormed up the aisle of the theater, and then disappeared from view.

I suddenly felt drained. I sat down on the floor inside the chalked square. It was only one week away from opening night, and even the sets weren't ready. A sense of unreality engulfed me. What was

I thinking? At the moment, the least of my problems was whether or not an imaginary character ever got to say his piece.

Hugh climbed onto the stage. Hands still resting casually in his pockets, he walked from one edge of the proscenium arch to the other. He paused to examine the ropes and sandbags heaped together in a jumble. He also examined the tattered canvas drop left over from some long-ago production, and he raised his eyes to inspect the beams and pulleys hanging high above. He seemed to be taking a leisurely tour, and meanwhile my life was in chaos.

At last, Hugh sat down beside me. He looked me over as if I were just one more theater prop. "I suppose it's a good thing I came in when I did," he said. "For being a married man, things were getting a little cozy up here, weren't they?"

I knew Hugh was trying to goad me. Worst of all, he was succeeding. I drew up my knees and wrapped my arms around them. "Don't be crass, Hugh. I've hurt Jason rather badly."

"So, tell me, Benny. Why didn't you marry him, instead of me?"

I had other questions on my mind, such as why I couldn't think straight whenever Hugh was near me like this. Hugh leaned back on one hand, his manner still casual. Unfortunately, there was nothing casual about my reaction to my new husband. I gazed at the strong lines of his features and felt a heat that had nothing to do with the glare of the theater lights.

I made an effort to concentrate on the subject of Jason. "The truth is, if I had any sense… well, I would have chosen him over you."

Hugh nodded thoughtfully. "Let's see…. You like him because he never shuts up. I seem to remember you saying something to that effect."

"Those weren't exactly the words I used." I tightened my arms around my knees. "Believe it or not, Hugh, I enjoyed being with a man who actually knew how to open up to me. A man who wasn't afraid to talk about his emotions or his thoughts. I need that in my life. It's something you can't seem to give to me."

We stared at each other. And this time, at least, I knew there was no mistaking the storminess in Hugh's eyes. Leaning toward me,

Hugh captured my mouth with his. It was an impertinent kiss, seeking and demanding a response. I wanted to resist. Dammit, why couldn't I resist?

But already my lips were pliant, accepting. I held my hand against Hugh's cheek, needing to touch him any way I could.

It seemed Hugh knew just what to do after that. He knew how to tantalize me by brushing his lips against the corner of my mouth, then deepening it all over again. A sensual game of retreat, advance, retreat again, until he compelled me to make my own urgent claims. Now I was the seeker, the one who demanded a response. Hugh complied willingly, but still he tantalized and enticed. Still he commanded my senses.

When at last we broke apart, I was breathing raggedly, the stage lights seeming to burn into me. Hugh's eyes were so dark they were almost black.

"Benny," he said huskily, his own breathing uneven. "Benny...."

I was trembling. And I could no longer deny the truth. No one else could make him feel this way. Not Jason, not anyone.

Because I loved Hugh.

I loved him completely, hopelessly. I'd tried to build a new life without him, but it hadn't worked. I could never escape my love for Hugh.

And so I'd married him again, this time for real, or rather, legally. The first time sure felt real enough, even if it hadn't been recognized by the state. And truth be told, it hadn't happened because of the champagne. It hadn't been just a wild impulse. I had known, deep down, that I had no other choice but to belong to Hugh.

The knowledge brought with it a terrible pain, because Hugh Bayard, my husband, could never truly love me in return.

CHAPTER TWENTY-ONE

MY SNEAKERS made no sound on the polished oak floor. For a second or two, I felt like a burglar who'd broken into this luxurious apartment. Yet, I held the key to it firmly in my hand. I had a right to be here.

I did a circuit of the spacious living room one more time. The hand-painted wallpaper was patterned in a graceful Chinese design of flowering branches. All the moldings were carved in an elaborate Baroque style, and the creamy marble pillars flanking the doorways were exquisitely veined. Because there was no furniture, the room was revealed in all its stately beauty.

I went to the window and gazed out over Central Park, where the treetops clustered in a vivid cushion of green. This was the Upper West Side, where everything about life was cushioned. This was where Hugh now expected me to live.

I perched on the window seat and turned the key over and over in my hand. Hugh amazed me. Not long ago, he had actually agreed with me when he said he thought Mother and Charles needed to start their marriage on neutral territory. But now, on his own, Hugh had chosen this apartment in Manhattan, deciding that he and I would live here. When we weren't spending time at his house in Charleston of course.

I curled my fingers around the key. It was happening all over again. It had been less than a week since that ill-fated trip to Las Vegas, but already Hugh had begun to take charge of my life and bend it to fit his own. This luxurious apartment was only one indication.

With an effort, I forced myself to relax. I set the key down, then leaned my forehead against the cool glass of the window. Unbidden, the events of last night came back to me.

Hugh had shown up without notice at my shabby little apartment. At first, I'd been happy to see him. I had shared my simple dinner with him—canned vegetable soup, bagels I'd bought at the bakery, a pint of cherry-cheesecake frozen yogurt. In a way, sharing that meal so unexpectedly had been romantic. And then... well, then we'd made love. I had given myself up to the magic of Hugh's embrace. The magic hadn't faded until afterward, when we'd lain spent together in my bed and once again Hugh had seemed to gaze right past me.

I pushed myself off the window seat. I could no longer bear to sit still. I paced through the rest of the elegant apartment. The master bedroom was quite grand with its Palladian windows and its balcony overlooking the park. This, of course, was where Hugh expected me to sleep with him. Hugh had no doubt chosen a king-size bed, where we wouldn't even have to touch after making love.

I folded my arms against my body as if that would somehow contain the ache of need and longing. Try as I might, I couldn't forget how it had been to wake up in my own small bed early this morning, only to find that Hugh was already gone. He'd left something on my bureau, a folded slip of paper with a terse message about the new home he'd acquired. Inside had been the key to this apartment. Why not just leave money the way he had the first time in New York? Payment for services rendered.

I couldn't stay here any longer. Beautiful as this apartment was, I detested it. It was too grand, too spacious, too elegant. I hurried toward the door.

I made the mistake of glancing into one more room. This one was clearly a nursery. A quaint border of fairy-tale figures had been painted along the walls—a pensive princess, a plump dragon, a knight on horseback.

Did Hugh expect this room to become our nursery? But I already knew the answer to that. He wanted children. He wanted someone who could carry on the Bayard tradition, the Bayard name. No doubt he still believed that I would be open to adopting or hiring a surrogate right away.

"No," I whispered, my throat tight. I turned away from the room and its impossibly naive fairy tales. "No, Hugh."

He wasn't here to listen. But when had he ever listened?

This time I walked straight to the front door of the apartment. I didn't even stop to pick up the key, left on the window seat. I just got out as quickly as he could.

"I'm in Paris! Benson, dear, can you believe it?"

"Paris," I echoed groggily, squinting at the clock by my bed. It was four o'clock in the morning New York time. I sank back against the pillow and cradled the phone against my ear. "Mother, I hate to ask this, but what on earth are you doing in Paris? You're supposed to be honeymooning in California."

"Well, that's just the thing. There we were, walking along the beach in Carmel when Charles asked me what I thought was the most romantic city in the world. Naturally, I said Paris, and the next thing I knew, Charles whirled me off to France. Isn't that incredible?"

"Actually, it is."

"Charles won't stop being romantic, Benson. It's the most amazing thing. He's taken the ball and run with it. I never know quite where I'm going to end up." Mary Grace sounded a little frazzled.

"Mother, are you all right?" I asked. I finally had my eyes completely open. Mary Grace's phone call had woken me from the first good night's sleep I'd had in a while.

"Of course, I'm all right. I'm in Paris, aren't I? With Charles. What more could I want?" Mary Grace did seem on edge.

"Be sure to get some rest," I said, stifling a yawn. "There's only so much romance you can take at one time."

For a moment, the line went quiet, filled with nothing but transatlantic static. Then Mary Grace spoke again, her voice muffled, as if she was cupping the receiver to avoid being overheard. "Well, that's just it. All these grand gestures can be a wee bit exhausting. Poor Charles, he has a dreadful case of jet lag. He's not accustomed to all this travel. Before, his idea of a trip was to go down to the garden center to check out the latest shipment of cucumber seed."

I smiled. "Still, you're in Paris, the most romantic city in the world."

"In other words," Mary Grace said tartly, "I shouldn't complain when I get what I ask for."

My sheet was tangled around my legs. I tried futilely to straighten it. "The problem with us is that we want perfection. Romance in just the right dose, not too much, not too little."

"Speaking of which, dear, how are you and Hugh getting along?"

I tensed. "I don't see what Hugh has to do with anything."

"Stop hedging, Benson. I saw how well the two of you were getting along at the wedding. Why not admit it?" It really seemed to perk Mary Grace up, talking about someone else's romance. But she didn't know the half of it. She didn't know what had happened after she and Charles left on their honeymoon.

I sat up in bed, rubbing my head. What was the use of trying to hide the truth? She would learn about it sooner or later—might as well be now.

"Mother… I suppose there's something I should tell you. While we were in Las Vegas, Hugh and I… well… we happened to, umm… visit the wedding chapel ourselves. On the spur of the moment, so to speak." I winced just at having to say the words out loud. Now there was more static on the line.

"Benson," Mary Grace said, sounding doubtful, "are you telling me what I think you're telling me?"

I grimaced. "I'm certainly not going to spell it out for you any further."

"Married? Oh my goodness! Put Hugh on." Mary Grace sounded shocked. I had expected exaltation.

I hesitated, staring at the empty pillow next to me. "Mother, most of us on this side of the ocean are still asleep. At least, we'd like to be asleep. Besides," I added in an acid tone, "Hugh isn't here."

"I thought something was amiss. Where on earth is he?"

I wished I'd never started this. I should have known better. Even from Paris, Mary Grace knew how to cause a stir.

"He's probably at home, Mother. His own home. In Charleston. And if he has any sense, he's asleep."

"At home? His home? What kind of marriage is this?" Mary Grace demanded. "Why, it's not right, Benson. Not right at all."

"Tell me about it," I said more bleakly than I'd intended.

"Dear me," Mary Grace muttered. "It really isn't right. Something has to be done. Something, indeed. Goodbye, Benson."

"Mother, wait—"

But Mary Grace had already hung up. The telephone line buzzed uselessly.

I dropped my cell on the bedside table. I was wide-awake now. I slipped out of bed and padded into the living room, almost tripping over the bike.

"Ouch." I switched on the light and sat down on the couch to examine my stubbed toe. I'd finally disposed of all the dead flowers, but the bicycle remained, taking up most of the space in the room.

I gazed at them for a long time. The one with the wire basket was a pretty shade of pale green. The other, somewhat larger, was slate black. It looked powerful and dynamic next to its more delicate companion.

Suddenly a wave of hopelessness washed over me. I pressed my hands against my eyes and slumped back against the couch.

My mother had asked the right question, the only question that mattered.

Just what sort of marriage was this?

I DRAGGED myself into the restaurant. I hadn't been able to go back to sleep after the call from Mother. I felt tired and depressed, the day seeming to stretch out gloomily before me: eight hours of work, then another rehearsal where Jason, in all his wounded dignity, would do his best to make me feel even guiltier. I would rather return to my apartment, crawl back into bed, and stay there for days. Unfortunately, the pre-lunch rush would be starting all too soon, and instead of doing what I wanted, I plastered on my mask of happy.

Melanie came striding into the work area. She gave me a quick nod, pulled on an apron, and began assembling the ingredients for side salads. There was something different about her today. She had a resolute expression on her face, but that wasn't all. The ponytail was back. No more carefully styled hair—just that no-nonsense, matter-of-fact ponytail.

"Want to talk about it?" I asked.

Melanie tore lettuce over a large mixing bowl. "There's not really anything to talk about."

"I think there is," I said quickly.

Melanie dropped the lettuce as if she'd suddenly lost her energy. She looked unhappy but very calm. Maybe too calm. "I broke it off," she said. "I ended it with Toby. I got caught up in the lust and the fantasy and… I took a step back, looked at it logically, and realized I didn't love him. So I ended it."

"I'm sorry you're hurting."

Melanie's face tightened for a moment. "I never was one to believe in fairy tales. I'll be fine."

Mel claimed she didn't believe in true love and happily ever after. I didn't believe her. I could see the pain the breakup caused her. She'd had her first taste of love and heartbreak. However, I also knew she'd be fine. She was one tough cookie.

"You're doing what's right for you," I said at last. "

Mel closed her eyes for a few seconds, then opened them again and gave me a sad smile. "Now I just need to convince my heart I did the right thing."

"I know how that is." I had learned too well how hard it was to convince your heart to listen to logic. An impossible task.

"Hugh?" Melanie asked gently.

I nodded. "Hugh."

"Want to talk about it?"

I attempted a light tone but wasn't successful. "Not much to talk about. I love him. It hurts."

"What a pair we are." This time, Mel's smile was genuine. "Think we could make a bigger mess of our lives if we tried?"

"Not likely. But there's at least one good thing in all this."

Melanie cocked her head. "What's that?"

"Your ponytail's back. I like it a lot."

CHAPTER TWENTY-TWO

I WAS petrified. A mere five minutes from now, I was expected to walk out onto the stage of the Stewart Mott Playhouse and pull off the part of Edgar. No more rehearsals. It was for real this time. Opening night. I stood in the wings, stone still, convinced I wouldn't be able to move at all when the time came. Five minutes to the first act. I wasn't ready!

Jason appeared beside me. "So far not much of an audience. I was afraid of this. The play could sink before it's even begun."

"Somehow, I don't find that reassuring," I muttered. I was ready to flee. It took everything in me to stand still when my mind was screaming *run, run, run*! Oh God, I was going to embarrass myself. A total flop. I scanned the area, looking for the closest exit.

"It could have been so different," Jason said from next to me. "You could have been with me, Ben, not your ex. Then we wouldn't give a damn what happened to the play. We'd have each other."

"Jason, please don't do this. Not here. Not now."

"I can't help it," Jason said. "Every time I look at you, I can't stop thinking of what could have been. What we could have been together."

"Jason, stop." My palms were sweating. My throat was dry. I was light-headed. What if I forgot my lines or lost my voice? What if I passed out?

"I don't know how I'm going to walk out on that stage and pretend you're someone named Edgar. I've been an actor for a long time, Ben, but I think this one's beyond me."

"Jason," I whispered fiercely, "I know you want me to realize just how miserable I've made you. Believe me, the message is getting through. But for right now, zip it!"

A slight smile curled Jason's lip. "You're no longer thinking about exiting stage left." Jason nodded toward the stage. "You can thank me later."

I glared at him, but there was no time to complain or slap him upside the head for messing with me. The tattered velvet curtains rose, and the lights sprang to life. Lindsey was already out there, lounging in an armchair, feet dangling over the side. It was actually a real armchair, not just a chalked square marked on the floor. Somehow, all the props had ended up ready on time after all.

Lindsey/Lori looked perfectly comfortable on stage, lolling as she glanced about the set. With just a few subtle techniques, she portrayed all the nuances of emotion. Her smile was that of someone secretly satisfied with herself; her leisurely posture conveying the inner confidence that was so much a part of Lori's character. Lindsey was a damn good actress. Far better than I could ever hope to be. This thought didn't do wonders for my confidence, which was already as tattered as the theater curtains.

Lindsey/Lori lazily changed position and stretched a little. My cue! And it was just as I'd feared. I was frozen. I couldn't move.

Jason nudged me forward. "You'll do great," he murmured. "Go out and knock 'em dead, Ben."

I gave Jason a startled glance. Now he decided to be encouraging? But his words seemed to do the job. At least I was walking out on stage, placing one foot in front of the other.

I couldn't see the audience beyond the footlights. It didn't matter, though. Just knowing people were out there was enough to send a jolt of fear through me all over again. Was Hugh part of the audience? He knew this was my big night, of course, but had he come? I was supposed to deliver my opening line. Why wouldn't my mouth open?

Lindsey/Lori gazed at me expectantly. I still couldn't get the words out. I knew what I was supposed to say, but I seemed to have forgotten the mechanics of speech. This was dreadful. It was terrible. I was going to disgrace myself entirely.

Lindsey/Lori did something quite unexpected then. She winked at me. It was the first time she'd evinced even a hint of camaraderie. But that was what this was all about, wasn't it? In spite of the wretched rehearsals, the arguments, the misunderstandings, Jason and Lindsey and I were in this play together. We could make it work, the three of us. I wasn't alone. Suddenly I found my voice.

"Lori, shouldn't you be doing something?"

"Something like what, Uncle Edgar?"

"Anything. You can't just sit around all day—"

"Pete will be here soon. Then I'll be doing something, won't I?"

Things weren't going too badly. Maybe they were even going okay. I started to loosen up a little. I just had to stop taking everything so seriously. So maybe I wasn't going to stun anybody with my acting ability tonight—I could live with that. As long as I really didn't forget my lines, and as long as I gave at least a hint of Edgar's character. No matter what, I knew Edgar—an intense, passionate, middle-aged man doing everything he could to combat loneliness—welcoming his niece and her boyfriend into his home, even as his paranoia threatened to overwhelm him. He wanted to have a relationship with at least one member of his family; only his passion for Pete, the secret smoldering between them, could ruin any chance of that happening.

Jason/Pete came onto the stage and the complications began to unfold—aimless Pete caught between self-involved Lori and self-tormented Edgar. I forgot about the audience. I even forgot to wonder if Hugh was out there watching. I got caught up in the story.

We made it through the first act, then to the middle of the second. Time seemed to race, and I could only hope I wasn't rushing my lines. But we were halfway through now. Surely I would make it the rest of the way.

Then came the moment in Act Two when Edgar was supposed to kiss Pete, and I found myself faltering. This was Jason I was supposed to kiss, a man who still professed to be in love with me. And if Hugh did happen to be watching.... *Shit!* I couldn't do this. I couldn't possibly pull it off. I couldn't pretend any longer that I was Edgar.

160

I had that awful sensation again, the one that had plagued me through so many rehearsals. It was as if I were watching the character of Edgar recede farther and farther from me, almost about to vanish. I couldn't catch up, couldn't grasp Edgar.

Jason/Pete stepped closer.

I/Edgar walked in front of the mantelpiece. "No," I said. "This isn't a good idea."

Jason/Pete took another step toward me. "Yes," he said. "You've been waiting for me to do this."

"I never wait, Pete. Not for anyone. Not for anything."

"Then maybe I'm the one who's been waiting." Jason placed his lips against mine.

I froze. Goddammit, I knew Hugh was watching. I could feel it. I was just going to stand there, as stiff and unconvincing as a washboard. I was going to ruin the play after all.

Then it happened.

Somehow, Edgar came back to me. I knew just what to do, just how to act. I lifted my hands and placed them on Jason's shoulders, returning the kiss. Except that, I didn't think of him as Jason anymore. He was Pete, my niece's boyfriend. Edgar felt guilty for kissing him, but he was also determined to take his chance while he could. The lights faded—end of Act Two.

And now it was the final act. The triangle of Pete and Lori and Edgar finally disintegrated. In the last scene, Edgar was alone, rejected by his lover, rejected by his niece.

The set was empty except for me/Edgar. I sank into the armchair facing stage right and gazed off into the distance. "I don't need either one of them. I don't need them at all." I bowed my head, the lights faded, and the curtains came creaking down.

Applause sounded from the audience. It wasn't overwhelming, but still, it was applause. Lindsey, Jason, and I did a curtain call—more applause, growing a bit in enthusiasm. And then Lindsey, undeniably the star of the show, took a curtain call on her own. Now the applause really got enthusiastic, with shouts of "Bravo!" That was fine with me. All I knew was that I'd made it through the play.

A happy and triumphant Lindsey actually gave me a hug. Then she gave Jason a hug. And then he gave me a hug.

"You did it," he said. "You were really good. And I'm not just telling you that because I'm in love with you."

"Jason—"

"I know. You're a married man now. And you want me to zip it." He released me and gave me a sorrowful smile.

Jason really did have a melodramatic streak. He was also endearing, in spite of those melodramatic tendencies. I felt a stirring of regret. Why couldn't I have fallen in love with Jason? It would have been so convenient. So safe.

Joyce came across the stage. She looked as world-weary as ever, her dyed red hair pushed back haphazardly from her face. She surveyed Lindsey, Jason, and me.

"None of you embarrassed me completely," she said grudgingly at last. "But you, Winthrop, you just had to play the part your way, didn't you?"

I gazed steadily at Joyce. "Believe it or not, I tried to play it both our ways."

"Hmph." It wasn't exactly approval, but it wasn't disapproval either.

I retreated to my dressing room after that, but I was not to be alone. The uncles had traveled all the way from Charleston for my opening night, and now they converged on me.

"Congratulations, my boy," said Uncle Johnathan. "I knew you would be a star someday."

"John, I believe I am the one who has always encouraged Benson in his artistic endeavors," Uncle Walt said.

"You, Walt? You never even knew our Benson wanted to be an actor."

"I am speaking of artistic endeavors in general."

"If it'd been up to you, Benson would have stayed in Charleston forever and never made a success of himself," Uncle Johnathan pointed out, a troublemaker's gleam in his eye.

"I want him to come home where he belongs, but I am still very proud of him," Uncle Walter said in a starchy voice.

I hugged each of them in turn. "If the two of you will stop arguing long enough, I'll tell you how much it means to me that you're here." I truly was delighted to see my uncles. They were my family, and the occasion wouldn't have been the same without them. I finally understood that family would always be important to me. Living away from Charleston this past year had taught me at least that much.

But even as I spoke to my uncles, I couldn't help looking past them to the door of the dressing room. I kept hoping and fearing that Hugh would show. Had he come to the play at all? Maybe it would be better if he hadn't. The person who next appeared at the door was none other than my mother, beaming on the arm of her new husband.

"Mother!" I exclaimed in surprise. "I thought you were in Paris. What on earth?"

She gave me a tight embrace. "I couldn't very well stay in France when you were having your debut, could I? You were wonderful, by the way, dear. Not that I would have expected any less. You're my son, after all."

"Thanks," I said wryly. It occurred to me that perhaps I had inherited any acting talent I had from my mother—the consummate manipulator of emotions.

"Besides," Mary Grace went on importantly, "I couldn't possibly stay in Paris when it's so clear you need my help with Hugh."

Speaking of manipulation. I struggled with the mixture of fondness and annoyance that Mary Grace always provoked in me. "I think Hugh and I will just have to work out our problems on our own, Mother."

"Nonsense."

She was prevented from saying more, because Charles stepped up to congratulate me himself. "You did an excellent job tonight. You should be proud of yourself," he said solemnly. Then he lowered his voice. "I can possibly arrange to fly your mother to Rome for a few weeks. I understand that's a romantic city too—"

"I can hear you," Mary Grace said imperturbably. "Charles, it's no use. I shall meddle in my son's life no matter where you whisk me off to." Then she was the one who lowered her voice confidentially as she leaned toward me. "I believe I have finally convinced Charles that we can be just as romantic at home as abroad. We can go for strolls together, watch old movies, that sort of thing. Small-scale romance, so to speak. Of course, we will be quite busy in the next few months, refurbishing the Bayard home. Hugh has decided to sell to us—but of course you knew that."

I hadn't known. Hugh hadn't shared that rather important piece of information with me. There was so much he didn't share.

"Well, we must all get out of here and leave Benson a few moments of peace," Mary Grace said, looking rather mysterious. "Come along. You both need to sit down."

"I'm hardly an invalid," grumbled Uncle Walter. "You don't need to mollycoddle me, Mary Grace."

"Speak for yourself, Walt," said Uncle Johnathan. "I like to be mollycoddled. Mollycoddle away."

"John, if you are trying to be snide about my choice of words...."

The small shabby dressing room seemed oddly lonely when everyone had finally exited. Hugh hadn't shown of course. I had refused to put myself through the humiliation of asking whether he'd even come.

I sat down in front of the makeup table, melancholy dampening my excitement. It was only now that I noticed flowers had been delivered sometime during the evening. A crystal vase stood on the table before me, filled with roses. I stared at the flowers, not quite daring to hope. Had Hugh sent them? I snatched the card lying nestled in the arrangement and scanned it eagerly.

My love endures, though you belong to another. To your happiness always.

I crumpled the card. Why did Jason have to keep behaving in this extravagant manner? I knew I'd hurt him, but Jason was turning himself into a martyr.

That wasn't what really disturbed me, though. I couldn't believe that once again I'd longed for something to be from Hugh, only to find out that it was from Jason instead. When would I stop hoping for all the things Hugh couldn't give?

"Hello, Benny."

I twisted around and saw him standing in the doorway. Hugh looked very elegant and commanding in a herringbone suit. My heartbeat quickened absurdly. I placed a hand to my chest as if that would somehow restrain my wayward pulse.

"Let me guess," I said as coolly as possible. "My mother sent you back here."

He came into the room. "Mary Grace likes to think she's orchestrating the world, but I'm actually here of my own volition."

"Well," I said stiffly, "did you enjoy the play?"

Hugh didn't answer for some moments, just gazed at me, his expression unreadable. What secrets did he really hide behind those dark eyes and obdurate features? Would he ever allow me to know?

"I thought you were sufficiently convincing in the role," Hugh said at last. Trust him not to overstate the case. I didn't have to worry about flattery where Hugh was concerned.

"Thank you, I suppose."

"You were particularly convincing in the scene where you kissed Collins."

"You're not going to start that again, are you? I'm playing a part. What happened between Jason and me is finished. If you can't realize that, then you don't know me very well at all. I've always been faithful to you. That hasn't changed, even though what we have can hardly be called a marriage." My tone was more bitter than I'd intended.

I twisted around again to face the pocked mirror. Taking a tissue, I began the process of wiping off my stage makeup. I needed a task to keep myself occupied, anything to prevent me from showing Hugh how much he affected me. How much I cared.

Hugh came to the table, picked up the crumpled card, and read it. "Collins just won't give up."

I felt compelled to defend Jason. "He's just being… theatrical."
"He's being a jerk," Hugh stated flatly.

Anger stirred inside me. "At least Jason isn't afraid to admit he feels things. And if he gets carried away with what he feels… well, at least he feels deeply enough to get carried away!"

"As opposed to me of course," Hugh said. "You believe I never get carried away."

"I don't just believe it, I know it." That melancholy settled deeper inside me. I knew Hugh's passion only when he took me to bed. Why couldn't Hugh give me the deeper passion I craved?

Hugh studied the vase with its arrangement of flowers. "I wanted to send you flowers of my own tonight," he said gruffly. "But I couldn't do it. I damn well couldn't celebrate you and Collins up there on the stage."

"Hugh, Jason isn't the problem between us. When will you realize that?"

I gave up the pretense of keeping busy. I pushed away the box of tissues and gazed at my reflection. My face was still streaked here and there with makeup, and I looked strangely mournful.

Hugh pulled over a chair and sat down next to me. "Somehow, I think Collins is the problem," he said. "I think, no matter what you say, that you keep comparing me to him. You've set him up as some knight in shining armor."

I felt that familiar ache, the one that had been with me for such a long time now. It had everything to do with Hugh and nothing to do with Jason. But how could I make Hugh understand?

"Hugh," I said carefully, "Jason isn't the man I want. I tried to make him be the one, but it just didn't work."

"I'm not the man you want, either, am I, Benny?"

The ache inside me constricted my heart. All I longed to do was go into Hugh's arms and tell him yes, yes, of course he was the man I wanted. The only man I wanted! But then everything would be the same as it had always been—Hugh leading, while I followed, my life revolving around Hugh's, my love for Hugh growing all the more, while he refused to love me in return.

I turned away from him. I turned away from the mirror, too, so that he wouldn't be able to see the yearning betrayed in my reflection. Did Hugh understand what my silence meant? He couldn't know. I clenched my hands tightly in my lap and kept my face averted.

Hugh shifted restlessly. "What will it take to make this marriage work?" he asked, sounding almost impatient. "We can't afford another failure, Ben."

I wondered if Hugh saw it only in those terms—failure or success. Didn't he view his business in much the same way? Something that could be measured through cost analysis, a certain amount of expenditures, a certain amount of profits. Did the benefits outweigh the costs?

I still refused to look at him. I knew I couldn't gaze into Hugh's eyes and still have the courage for what I needed to say.

"I can't go back," I said in a low voice. "I can't let our marriage be what it was. You have to offer me more, Hugh. You have to decide you're really going to share a life with me. You have to give me as much as I'm willing to give you. Most of all, you have to let me into your heart. I can't accept anything less."

Hugh was silent for a while but then said, "You make it sound like an ultimatum."

How coldly he could speak, allowing no emotion to surface in his voice. Well, I had to be cold now too. I had to be strong. "It is an ultimatum. No compromises this time, no half measures."

I clenched my hands even more tightly, waiting for Hugh's answer. This was his chance to give me what I required—maybe his last chance. But would he take it?

Please, please, Hugh, be who I need.

His answer came. No words were necessary. He simply stood, remained completely still for a moment, and then walked from the dressing room. He closed the door after him, the only sound the slight click of the latch.

Left alone, just as Edgar had been alone at the end of the play. But this time my emotions didn't belong to an imaginary character.

This time my heart was truly breaking.

167

CHAPTER TWENTY-THREE

SOMEONE WAS pounding on my door. I pulled the pillow over my head, determined to ignore it. I was exhausted. Last night was the fourth night in a row I'd performed the role of Edgar. Staying in character, building the emotions necessary throughout the play, required far more from me than I ever imagined. Today, thank goodness, was my day off from the Common Cure. I needed to sleep. I did not need to answer that obnoxious banging at my door.

Whoever it was wouldn't let up. A knock came, then a pause, then another knock. It was almost getting into a sort of rhythm.

Oh for Christ's sake, I finally crawled out of bed. I pulled my robe on and stalked into the living room.

"Who is it?" I called grumpily.

"Special delivery" came a very identifiable voice from the other side of the door—the voice of Hugh Bayard—my husband.

I froze. I couldn't possibly let him in. If I did, I'd lose the little equanimity I'd been able to achieve these past few days. It would be the worst thing I could do for myself.

"Benny, I need to talk to you."

"Why?" I demanded. "Why now?"

"Why not now?" Hugh countered.

I hesitated. Hugh was so close, just on the other side of the door. But physical proximity wasn't what I needed from him. If I was smart, I'd leave all the bolts firmly in place. I'd go back to my solitary bed and hide under my pillow again.

"Benny," Hugh murmured.

Why did he have to say my name like that, his voice lingering on each syllable with just a trace of huskiness?

I undid the bolts and opened the door a crack. I peered out.

Hugh stood there gazing back at me. His expression was intense, his dark hair a little rumpled as if he'd been running his hands through it. I felt myself go weak with the longing to touch him. A tingling went through me, as if only near Hugh did I truly come to life. It wasn't fair, Hugh being here like this, disrupting my life once more. I pulled my robe tighter around me. Why, I'm not sure. A barrier perhaps? I don't know. I wished desperately I could just shut the door again.

"What do you want, Hugh? What's this all about?"

"You'd better let me in. I have something to tell you, Benny," he said with determination. "Make that a lot of things."

I hesitated another moment and then reluctantly pulled the door open wider. That was all the invitation Hugh needed. He came into my apartment, walked around the bicycle, and sat down on the couch. He still looked very intense.

"Have a seat," he said.

Only Hugh could barge in here and tell me to have a seat as if he owned the place. Hugh fished in the back pocket of his pants and brought out a rather creased slip of paper. He opened it and glanced over it with a frown. "I have a lot to say," he repeated. "Number one—"

"You brought a list?" I asked in disbelief.

Hugh looked disgruntled. "Yes, I have a list. It's not every day I go spouting off at the mouth, and I could use a little help. Sort of a cheat sheet. Is that so bad?"

I was confused, battling any number of stubborn hopes. I went to sit on the far end of the couch. "I suppose I'm ready."

Hugh rattled his list, then studied it for a long moment. "Hell," he said, sounding disgusted. "It isn't going to work. I'm no good at this, Benny. I came here so I could do what you're always asking. I came here to open up. I just don't know how to go about it."

Those stubborn hopes of mine were growing stronger. "Maybe I could help," I said. "Maybe you could show me the list, and we could go from there."

"Maybe." Hugh didn't sound convinced, but he handed the sheet of paper to me.

I examined it carefully. Hugh's writing was aggressive and hard to decipher. Several words had been crossed out, others jotted in. I examined it a moment longer, then glanced at him. "There's only one problem—for the life of me, I've never been able to read your handwriting. Maybe if you could just... start at the beginning."

Hugh balanced his elbows on his knees and gazed broodingly at the floor. He seemed to be thinking things over. "The beginning... I don't know where that is. Lord, Benny, all I can think about right now is the year I turned seventeen. So long ago. It should be done with. It should be finished. I was just a boy; I'm not anymore. I'm forty now. A different person. Hell, at least I *should* be different."

I listened intently. I heard the pain he was struggling so hard to stifle. Just as he was clearly trying to stifle the seventeen-year-old boy he'd once been.

I wanted to reach out to him. But some instinct warned me not to speak but to listen.

"I was seventeen," Hugh said, his voice very low. "Everything changed that year. My mother was diagnosed with cancer. That only made the problems between my parents worse. They didn't know how to face her illness, how to pull together against it. My father started spending more and more time away from home, flying in that old seaplane he loved. He was trying to escape, I suppose, just like I'd always tried to escape that house. Then his plane crashed."

I had only been nine at the time of Alexander Bayard's death, but I could still remember standing on the front lawn early one morning with my parents and great-uncles, all of them shocked because they'd just learned the news—Hugh's father had crashed in his plane and died instantly.

Hugh stood up abruptly. He glanced toward the door as if he wanted more than anything to bolt. I had to force myself to stay seated where I was, letting him decide what he would do.

"Benny," he said, his voice very heavy now, "I felt so damn guilty. There'd been times I'd wished both of my parents would go away, disappear somehow. Then my mother became ill, and my father died. I kept thinking that if I'd just done something differently, he'd still be alive. She wouldn't be sick."

Hugh's features tensed, as if he were still struggling to keep all the pain inside. "My mother would be lying there in the house, in her sick room, and she'd call for me. She'd send the nurse away and call for me instead. Of course, I went to her, I always went. How could I not? She was my mother. She was sick. She was dying. I remember the smell of that room. Lord, Benny… all the cleaning, all the disinfecting in the world, couldn't hide that smell. The smell of sickness, of dying. As if her soul were decaying right there before me. Her soul, not just her body."

Hugh sat down again. He stared straight ahead, and when he spoke again, his voice was devoid of all emotion. "She wanted me to be there beside her. She wanted me to tell her about all the good times, all the wonderful times we'd had as a family. Happy memories, that was what she wanted to hear. I tried. God, I tried. But there were no happy memories. So my mother let me know the good times had happened before I came along. She told me that she and my father had been very happy but only before me. I can still hear her voice. Plaintive. Angry, asking me why I'd come between them. Why I'd made them hate each other. Over and over, she asked me that, demanding an answer. What answer could I give her? When I couldn't listen anymore, I'd leave. But she'd call for me again. The next day and the day after. And I'd go to her again. She was my mother. I had to go to her."

I felt a chill deep inside. How little I had known of Hugh's family. Images of Grace Bayard flashed before my eyes—a frail woman sinking into her illness. A delicate woman, it had seemed. Yet she had lashed out at her only son, blaming him for her suffering. Perhaps she simply hadn't been strong enough to blame herself. How terrible to be so weak that you would turn on your own child. Hugh was right: Grace Bayard had been sick in her soul, far more than in her body.

"Day after day," Hugh said, his voice still expressionless. "Day after day. For a year, it was like that. A year until she died. I'd never realized how many days there were in a year. All those days to wonder if it'd been my fault. Wondering if everything bad in my family somehow did revolve around my existence."

I could no longer restrain myself. I went to him. I sat close and wrapped my arms around him as tightly as I could. Hugh was motionless for a very long moment. But then he brought his own arms around me, holding me close.

"God, Benny, can you imagine what it feels like to be glad when your mother finally dies? To be relieved that she's gone? And then to know more damn guilt because of it?"

"It's all right," I whispered. "It's okay. You're not to blame for anything that happened." I was trying to comfort the seventeen-year-old boy, the boy he'd once been. Maybe that was impossible. He was a man now, maturity forged on that long-ago pain. I didn't know how much I could help. But I went on holding him, anyway, and being held in return.

We stayed like that on the couch in my shabby little apartment for a very long while, wrapped in each other's arms. Finally, Hugh met my gaze. His features were still tense. "I'm sorry, Benny, for what I put you through. After my mother died, it seemed I'd had enough emotion to last a hundred lifetimes. I guess I had to protect myself somehow, so I never gave you what you needed. I shut myself off. I'm still shutting myself off."

"No, you're not. You're here with me now. You came to me, Hugh. Whatever happens from now on, you came to me. If you could just tell me one more thing—"

"I love you, Benny. I love you with all my heart. Do you know how much it scares me to say that?"

I closed my eyes and rested my head against his cheek. Oh, what a journey it had been. I felt as if I had traveled all my life just to hear Hugh say those words.

"What happened with your parents won't happen with us," I said softly. "I promise you that. You can let go with me, Hugh. You can trust me."

Hugh lifted my chin and gazed at me fully. "To think I almost lost you." The emotion in his statement was evident in the husky tone of his voice. "I've been so damn stubborn, so determined not to let down my guard. It's not going to be easy, learning how after all this time. Will you have patience with me?"

"Yes. Oh yes, as long as you love me," I said fervently.

"I love you, Benny. Lord, I always have. I just wouldn't admit it. Can you forgive me for that?" His eyes were very dark.

I placed my fingers tenderly against his lips. "No more guilt, not between the two of us. I love you, Hugh. I've loved you all my life. And now I love you even more—"

Hugh pressed his lips to mine, demanding entrance. I happily opened up to him, giving myself over. It was a kiss of promise, of renewal.

EPILOGUE

I LAY in Hugh's arms, warm and replete. He smoothed damp strands of hair away from my face.

"That was great," he said. "It always is with you, Benny."

I reached up and teasingly stroked his jaw. "We just happen to be very good in bed together. What can we do about it?"

"Just stay in practice, that's all I can say."

I smiled softly. "You never look away anymore."

Hugh gave me a quizzical look. "I'm not sure I know what you mean."

But maybe there wasn't really any need for me to explain. Somehow, during this past year of our new marriage, it had happened naturally. Hugh would make love to me, and afterward I would still see all the love from Hugh's heart showing in his eyes. Just as I was seeing it now.

Not that revealing his emotions came easily. He still withdrew from time to time behind the wall he'd found necessary to build in his childhood and beyond. But he and I were working on taking it down brick by brick. Maybe we would be working at it the rest of our lives. That would be all right as far as I was concerned. I knew that I was safe and cherished in Hugh's love, even when he couldn't always express it.

"Meow."

I peered over the edge of the bed at the spoiled glossy-black cat. A pair of yellow eyes stared at me accusingly.

"Okay, okay," I grumbled. "I'll feed you, Sidney."

Before I could slip from the bed, Hugh grabbed me by placing a possessive hand on my shoulder and kissing the nape. "Where do you think you're going?"

"King Sidney has spoken."

"But I'll miss you," Hugh said. He kissed his way down to the center of my back. I shuddered.

"If you keep that up, the cat is never going to get his tuna."

Hugh looped his arms gently around me and cradled me against his chest. "Who's more important, me or the cat?"

"Well…," I teased, but I didn't try to escape Hugh's warm embrace. During the past year, Hugh had done a very good job of showing me just how much love we had between us.

"Meow!"

"Okay, okay," Hugh grumbled. "Breakfast."

I laughed. Yup, we had a lot of love between us, and it was a good thing too, because the little cat demanded a whole lot of it.

Hugh pulled on his sweatpants and led the way to the kitchen, the cat slinking along behind him. I pulled on my robe and followed a moment later. I paused in the living room, glancing around at the clutter. Two bicycles, for rides in Central Park, were propped in the corner. The one with a wire basket was a pretty shade of light green, and the other was slate black. I liked having the bicycles right here, but one of these days, I'd get around to organizing the rest of the place. I was still a rotten housekeeper. So was Hugh. But, a little at a time, we were decorating this Greenwich Village townhouse we'd purchased together. And whenever we had a chance, we worked on the house in Charleston too. It was still quite difficult to get Hugh into an antique store, but I was doing my best.

I went to stand by the window and allowed the summer sunshine to wash over me. What a complicated life Hugh and I had chosen to live. We'd chosen to juggle two homes, along with the beach house, two careers, and a very demanding little cat. But somehow, we managed it. We'd come this far. Hugh still worked long hours, but not nearly as long as he had during our first marriage. He was getting better at delegating authority and making compromises so he and I could be together.

I pressed my forehead against the window, smiling ruefully. I was getting better at making compromises too. It had just taken me a while to realize I, too, needed to make a few changes. I'd finally quit my job at the restaurant, accepting that independence came in many shapes and forms—accepting also that I only had so much time in the day. If I wanted to have time for my husband, see my family in Charleston, continue acting classes, go to auditions, and go sailing with Hugh, then something had to give.

The second time around was even better than the first. Hugh wasn't as romantic as I had once hoped. We had different definitions of romance, but we were meeting in the middle, and it was pretty damn good there. Plus, I could finally trust Hugh with my heart and my dreams. Maybe it was time to make another dream come true and start thinking seriously about providing Sidney with someone else to bow down to him. I was beginning to think having a family, hearing the pitter-patter of little feet—human feet—was exactly what we needed to complete our lives.

While Sidney ate his tuna, Hugh stood beside me at the window and linked our fingers.

"Happy?" he asked.

I squeezed Hugh's hand and looked up into his eyes. "Ridiculously so."